we

are

all

made

of

molecules

ALSO BY SUSIN NIELSEN

The Reluctant Journal of Henry K. Larsen

Dear George Clooney: Please Marry My Mom

Word Nerd

we
are
all
made
of
molecules

SUSIN NIELSEN

WENDY
LAMB
BOOKS

Text copyright © 2015 by Susin Nielsen
Jacket art copyright © 2014 by Minna So

All rights reserved. Published in the United States by Wendy Lamb Books,
an imprint of Random House Children's Books, a division of Random House LLC,
a Penguin Random House Company, New York.

Wendy Lamb Books and the colophon are trademarks of Random House LLC.

Visit us on the Web! randomhousekids.com
Educators and librarians, for a variety of teaching tools,
visit us at RHTeachersLibrarians.com

Library of Congress Cataloging-in-Publication Data
Nielsen-Fernlund, Susin.
We are all made of molecules / Susin Nielsen. — First edition.
pages cm
Summary: Thirteen-year-old brilliant but socially-challenged Stewart and mean-girl
Ashley must find common ground when, two years after Stewart's mother died, his
father moves in with his new girlfriend—Ashley's mother, whose gay ex-husband lives
in their guest house.
ISBN 978-0-553-49686-4 (trade) — ISBN 978-0-553-49687-1 (lib. bdg.) —
ISBN 978-0-553-49688-8 (ebook) — ISBN 978-0-553-49689-5 (pbk.)
[1. Interpersonal relations—Fiction. 2. Family problems—Fiction. 3. High schools—
Fiction. 4. Schools—Fiction. 5. Bullies—Fiction. 6. Dating (Social customs)—Fiction.
7. Gay fathers—Fiction. 8. Moving, Household—Fiction.] I. Title.
PZ7.N565We 2015
[Fic]—dc23
2014017652

The text of this book is set in 11.75-point Fairfield.
Interior design by Heather Kelly

Printed in the United States of America
10 9 8 7 6 5 4
First Edition

TO OSKAR—BOY, DID DAD
AND I HIT THE JACKPOT.

STEWART

I HAVE ALWAYS wanted a sister.

A brother, not so much. I like symmetry, and I always felt that a sister would create the perfect quadrangle or "family square," with the X chromosomes forming two sides and the Ys forming the rest.

When I bugged my parents, they would say, "Stewart, we already have the perfect child! How could we do any better than you?" It was hard to argue with their logic.

Then one day, when I had just turned ten, I overheard a private conversation between them. I was in my room building my birthday present, an enormous Lego spaceship, without using instructions, because I have very good spatial abilities. My mom and dad were downstairs, but I could hear their voices clearly through the heating vent.

"Leonard," I heard my mom say, "Stewart might finally get his wish." I put down my Lego pieces and moved closer to the vent. "I haven't had my period in two months. I'm chubbing up around the middle. I'm tired all the time. . . ."

"You think you're pregnant?" I heard my dad say.

"I do."

I couldn't help myself. "FINALLY!" I yelled through the vent. "BEST BIRTHDAY PRESENT EVER!"

The next day, Mom made an appointment with her doctor.

But it wasn't a baby growing inside her. It was cancer. It had started in her ovaries, and by the time they caught it, it had spread.

She died a year and three months later.

Now I'm thirteen, and I still miss her like crazy, because she was a quality human being. When I was seven, my dad and I bought her a mug for her birthday that read WORLD'S BEST MOM, and I actually believed there was only one mug like it on the planet, and that it had been made just for her.

I don't like to talk a lot about the year she was sick. Or the year after she died. My dad is also quality and he did his best, and I like to think that I am quality and so I did my best, too. But it was really hard because we were missing one-third of our family.

We had been like an equilateral triangle.

Mom was the base that held up the whole structure. When we lost her, the other two sides just collapsed in on each other.

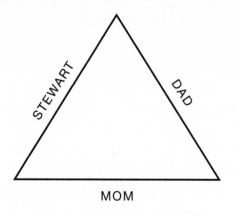

STEWART DAD MOM

We were very, very sad. My therapist, Dr. Elizabeth Moscovich, told me early on in our sessions that a part of us will always be sad, and that we will have to learn to live with it. At first I thought she wasn't a very good therapist, because if she was good she should be able to cure me. But after a while I realized that the opposite was true: she's an excellent therapist, because she tells it like it is.

Dr. Elizabeth Moscovich also says that just because you feel sad sometimes, it doesn't mean you can't also be happy, which at first might sound like a serious contradiction. But it's true. For instance, I can still be happy when Dad and I see a ball game at Nat Bailey Stadium. I can still be happy when I am kicking my best friend Alistair's butt at Stratego. And when Dad and I adopted Schrödinger the cat from the SPCA last year, I wasn't just happy; I was over the moon.

Of course, Schrödinger's not even close to a replacement for my mom. He can't have good conversations; he can't cook my favorite from-scratch chicken fingers; he can't give me back tickles or kiss my forehead at night. But he needs me, and I need him. He needs me to feed him and cuddle him and scoop his poops. I need him to talk to, even though he never talks back. And I need him to sleep by my head at night, because then I don't feel alone.

So when Dad started to date Caroline Anderson a year after Mom died, I mostly understood. Caroline is Dad's Schrödinger. He needs her and she needs him. It doesn't mean he isn't still sad sometimes, because he is. But it means he can put the sad on hold for bigger periods of time, and this is a good thing. For a long time he was Sad Dad twenty-four-seven, and I was Sad Stewart twenty-four-seven, and together we were Sad Squared, and it was just a big black hole of sadness.

Caroline and my dad have worked together in the newsroom for almost ten years. They'd always got along, but it wasn't until they were both single that they started to notice each other *in that way*. Caroline's husband left around the time my mom died. She is a *divorcée*. I'd met her a few times when Mom was still alive, at Dad's work parties. And of course I see her on TV all the time. I like her, and she likes me. Even better, she liked my mom, and I know the feeling was mutual.

But most important of all, she loves my dad. I can see it in the way she looks at him all google-eyed, and he looks at her the same way. Sometimes it makes my stomach hurt when I think about my mom, and how, if things had been different, *she* would be getting Dad's google-eyes, but as Dr. Elizabeth Moscovich has pointed out, I can't live in the past. Caroline makes my dad happy, and this is a good thing.

Best of all, she has a daughter. Her name is Ashley, and

she is one year older than me. I have only met Ashley a few times. She is very pretty, but I think she is also possibly hard of hearing, because when I try to talk to her, she either walks away or turns up the volume on the TV really loud.

Maybe she's just shy.

And now we are moving in with them. Dad and Caroline broke the news last month. Dad and I and Schrödinger are leaving our house in North Vancouver and moving into Caroline and Ashley's house in Vancouver, on Twenty-Second between Cambie and Main. They told Ashley and me separately, so I don't know her reaction, but I am 89.9 percent happy with the news.

"Eighty-nine point nine?" Dr. Elizabeth Moscovich asked me at our final session last week. "What about the other ten point one percent?"

I confessed to her that that part is made up of less positive emotions. We made a list, and on the list were words like *anxiety* and *guilt*. Dr. Elizabeth Moscovich told me this was perfectly normal. After all, we're leaving the house I spent my entire life in, the one Mom and Dad bought together a year before I was born. Now Dad has sold the house to a young couple with a baby, which means there is no turning back. We're bringing a lot of stuff with us, but we can't bring the mosaic stepping-stones my mom made that line the path in the backyard, or the flowers she planted, or her molecules, which I know still float through the air, because why else can I feel her presence *all the time*? It is what less scientifically minded people would call a "vibe," and our house, even this long after her death, is still full to bursting with Mom's vibe.

I worry a little bit about that. Where will her vibe go when we are gone? Will it find its way to our new home, like those animals that walked hundreds of miles to find their owners in *The Incredible Journey*? Or will it get lost on the way?

And also I am anxious because I don't know how Ashley feels about this merger of our family and hers. I don't expect her to be 89.9 percent excited. I just hope she's at least 65 percent excited. I can work with 65 percent.

This is not how I wanted my wish to come true. This is not how I would have chosen to become a quadrangle. I would far, far rather still be a triangle if it meant that my mom was alive. But since that is a scientific impossibility, I am trying to look on the bright side.

I have always wanted a sister.

And I'm about to get one.

ASHLEY

MY FAMILY IS FUBAR.

That's the word my part-time friend Claudia used to describe her own family at school yesterday. I said I didn't have a clue what that meant, and she said, "That makes sense, 'cause you're clueless." Then she told me it's a military term. It's short for "Effed Up Beyond All Recognition," except in the military, they don't say "effed."

See, Claudia has been in a so-called blended family for a few years now. She has a wicked stepfather and two snotty-nosed little half sisters. So she totally gets the insanity that is about to happen to me.

I am only just-turned-fourteen, so Claudia says I have to wait another two years before I can hire a lawyer and get unconstipated. Wait. That's not right. I keep having to look it up. I mean *emancipated*. According to Claudia, it means you can divorce your parents and be free of them for good. Claudia wants to divorce her family, too. So even though she's a little chunky around the middle and doesn't wash her hair enough and is not even close to my social status, she does kind of get what I'm going through.

What really bugs me, though, is that my family wasn't always FUBAR. For twelve and a half years it was perfect. My dad works at an advertising agency, and my mom anchors the local evening news. They are both very good-looking for old people, and I'm not being arrogant but just stating a fact when I say I inherited the best from both of them. We have an almost-new silver Volvo station wagon, and until a year and a half ago we took a trip to Maui every March break. We have a big modern house with another, miniature house in the backyard that's called a laneway home. Laneway homes are all the rage in Vancouver. They're built beside the alleys that run behind our houses, where a garage would normally go. We had ours built just before my world came crashing down around my feet. My parents thought that maybe they would rent it out for a few years, then I could live in it if I went to university in Vancouver, even though my ninth-grade counselor says I need to "face the cold, hard truth" because a C average will not get me into university.

Again, I am just stating a fact when I say that my friends were jealous of me and my life. And I couldn't blame them in the slightest. I would have been jealous of my life, too, if it hadn't already been mine.

Then, a year and a half ago, my dad sat my mom down and said the two words that tore our family to shreds.

"I'm gay."

None of my friends know that part. Not even my best friend, Lauren. I just told her my parents split because they were fighting all the time.

'Cause, see, there are Certain People who have this idea that I'm not a nice person. This is totally untrue and false and a lie. But Certain People think I'm a Snot (at least, that's what some jerk wrote on my locker in eighth grade). Claudia told me Certain People were actually pleased when my parents split up, like I somehow deserved a little pain. I guess it is somewhat partially halfway true that I have made a few comments over the years about other people's families (like, I might have told Violet Gustafson her mother was a skank before Violet broke my nose, which has fortunately healed so well you can hardly notice), but my comments were misunderstood. When I said that to Violet, I meant it more as an observation than an insult. But Violet and her friend Phoebe didn't see it that way, so now I call them Violent and Feeble behind their backs, which I personally think is quite clever.

So I didn't get an ounce of sympathy from anyone when my parents split. In fact, I got a lot of smirks from Certain People when they found out. Even Lauren's sympathy seemed awfully phony, which I admit really hurt. That's why there is no way I'm telling anyone the gay part. Not because Certain People are gayists (although I'm sure some of them are), but because they would *love* the fact that my so-called perfect life was built on one gigantic lie.

I guess, if I'm totally one hundred percent honest, I'm a bit gayist, too. I didn't think I was. I mean, I love Geoffrey, my mom's hair-and-makeup guy in the newsroom, and he is gay. And I see gay people on my favorite TV shows, and they seem cheerful and snarky and fun to be around.

But it's different when your dad suddenly announces he *is* one. There is nothing cheerful or fun about that. It opens up a lot of questions. Questions that I don't really want to know the answers to. Questions like: *Did you ever really love us? Or was that a lie, too?*

MY DAD TOLD MY mom he was gay on a Tuesday. By Saturday he had moved out.

Not to an apartment downtown. Not to Siberia, as I'd suggested.

Nope. He moved approximately six feet away from us, into our laneway house.

!!!!!!!!!!!!!!!!!!!!

My newly gay dad couldn't afford to get his own place unless he and Mom sold the house, which they both agreed would be too hard on me. So their genius solution: let him live in our backyard. Like, if I look out *our* kitchen window, I look into *his* kitchen window.

At first I figured it was just temporary. I figured Mom and I would bond over our hatred of Dad, and pretty soon our combined anger would force him to move out, and we would never have to see him again.

No such luck. Not only is he still living there, but Mom totally betrayed me. First, she just couldn't stay mad at Dad. They are actually "working on being friends" now!!!! Second, she started dating her producer, Leonard Inkster, a year ago, which I am pretty sure breaks all kinds of workplace rules.

And third—as if tearing out my heart and smashing it to the ground repeatedly wasn't enough—my mom has asked Leonard to move in with us. And Leonard doesn't come alone. He comes with his midget-egghead-freakazoid of a son.

Oh my God. Their moving van is pulling up right now.

I hate my mom.

I hate my dad.

I hate Leonard.

I hate his kid.

I hate my life.

Two more years till I can get unconstipated.

STEWART

MY DAD AND I moved in all our things in just under two hours. We were fast because we'd already put a lot of stuff into a storage locker last week. I wasn't very happy about this, but Dad reminded me that Caroline already has a house full of furniture, and we can't have two of everything. This makes a lot of sense on a practical level, and Dad and I are both very practical. But it is an interesting biological conundrum when one organ—in this case, my brain—tells me one thing, and another organ—in this case, my heart—tells me another.

So I cannot tell a lie: it didn't feel good, filling up that locker with the things that represented our entire life with Mom. Like the Formica kitchen table with gold sparkles where the three of us sat for most of our meals. Or the couch with the red-and-yellow flowers where Mom lay when she had bad days, trying to knit if she had the energy. Or the coffee table with circular stains all over it because Mom didn't believe in coasters. I got a little choked up when Dad closed the door, even though he promised me we could visit anytime we want.

I cheered myself up with the thought that we still had a van full of belongings. Some of it was stuff Dad and I had agreed on, like the *Mother and Child* painting my mom had done in one of her art classes. And Dad also let me pick three things just for me. I chose (1) the afghan blankets she knitted, one for my room and one for the back of our couch, (2) the big, overstuffed green-and-purple chair where she'd read me all the Harry Potter books, and (3) her collection of ceramic figurines.

Caroline was outside to greet us when we pulled up. She wore jeans and a sweatshirt, and her long red hair was pulled back in a ponytail. She is very pretty and also very nice. "Welcome!" she said, and she gave me a big hug and a kiss, even before she hugged and kissed my dad. "We're so happy you're here."

Because she had used the word *we,* I asked, "Where's Ashley?"

Caroline hesitated. "She's in her room. She has a lot of studying to do." I had heard from my dad that Ashley doesn't do well in school, so this made sense.

"All right, everyone, time for some heavy lifting," Dad said. He posed like a bodybuilder and grunted, which made Caroline laugh.

The three of us unloaded the van. I brought Schrödinger up to my new room, which used to be the guest bedroom.

It's big but bland; the walls are beige, whereas at home—I mean, the place where I used to live until today—Mom and I had painted my walls bright blue. I let Schrödinger out of his carry cage and put him into the en suite bathroom so he wouldn't escape while we carried everything in, or pee on the carpet.

I confess it gave me quite a thrill to realize I would have my own bathroom. At home—I mean, the place where I used to live until today—we only had one bathroom. This house has *five*! One for Caroline and Dad, one for Ashley, one for me, one on the main floor that's just a toilet and a sink, and another full one in the basement! Every single human member of this household could go at the same time and there would still be a bathroom left over.

When I closed the door behind Schrödinger, I spotted an enormous box of Purdy's Chocolates perched on the window ledge. Purdy's are the best. There was a note attached that said, *We are so happy that you are joining our family. Love, Caroline and Ashley.* I got a little choked up.

I ate six chocolates before leaving my new room. On the way to the stairs, I passed Ashley's room, which is at the other end of the hall. Her door was closed. I thought about knocking to thank her for the chocolates, and maybe even offer her one, but I wasn't sure if I should interrupt her studying. So I didn't.

THE ANDERSON HOUSE IS very different from the Inkster house, and not just because it has so many toilets. First of all, it is much more modern. Our house—I mean, the house where I lived until today—was old. It was built in the 1940s, and it was a bungalow, and the rooms were small and the floors creaked. This house is very big and very clean and very clutter-free. I would call their style *minimalist,* whereas our house was *maximalist.* We had stuff everywhere! There were books stacked on tables and on the floor, and at least one of my school projects was always spread out on the dining room table. We must have had about twenty houseplants. Paintings and family photos covered the walls. Mom's ceramic figurines lined the mantel over the fireplace and every windowsill on the main floor. Plus there was her knitting, her drawing pencils, her notepads, her long-forgotten half-full mugs of tea, her magazines, Dad's newspapers and reading glasses, his dirty socks and mine, plus my chemistry set and comics.

So I figure we're doing them a favor, adding some of our stuff to the mix; it will help make their house look more lived-in. For example, we placed the big green-and-purple armchair between their slender brown leather couch and two matching brown leather club chairs in the family room. It was a tight squeeze, but it livened up the space immediately, if I do say so myself. I threw one of my mom's afghans on the back of their couch, which added a much-needed splash of color. And I see at least five good spots to hang Mom's painting, and plenty of places to display her ceramic figurines.

Once, when I was out by the van, I caught a glimpse of Ashley. She was standing at her bedroom window, gazing down at us. I waved. She didn't wave back.

Maybe she isn't just hard of hearing. Maybe she's hard of seeing, too.

ASHLEY

MOM FORCED ME TO come downstairs for supper. I was in my bedroom, sketching an idea for a new outfit instead of doing math, when she knocked. I didn't answer, so she spoke through the door. "Ashley, I want you to join us at the table."

"I'm busy."

I could hear her sigh. "I expect you to eat with us. And I expect you to be pleasant."

"No on both counts."

"Ashley, you're pushing your luck."

"I never wanted them to move here in the first place. I'm a part of this family, too, and my vote didn't even count."

Then Mom opened my door because there is no lock on it even though I have asked for one. I have *no privacy*

16

whatsoever. "When you buy your own house and start paying the mortgage on that house, you will have a vote," she said. "Until then, you will stop whining and do as you're told."

Sometimes my mother is like the queen in *Snow White*—beautiful but oh-so-cold.

I crossed my arms over my chest. "I'm not coming down."

"Fine," she said in her fake-reasonable voice. "But if you don't, you will not get your allowance this week."

So unfair! I am *this close* to being able to afford an amazing skirt I saw at H&M, and she knows it. "You are so *evil*," I said as I stood up to follow her.

"Yup. I'm right up there with Idi Amin and Slobodan Milosevic."

I have no idea who she was talking about. Probably a couple of guys from work.

WHEN I GOT DOWNSTAIRS, the freakazoid was already at the table. I sat down across from him and gave him the once-over in a very obvious way.

He is a seriously funny-looking kid. He has a mass of thick, unruly brown hair that is neither straight nor curly. It's cut short, which only accentuates his sticky-outy ears. But even though it's short, there's still so much of it, like he has a furry rodent perched on top of his head. And speaking of short: he is. I wanted to offer him a booster seat.

"Hi, Ashley," he said as I sat down.

"Hi, Spewart."

"Actually, it's Stewart." He shouted this, like I was deaf or something.

Mom came in from the kitchen, carrying a salad. She was followed by Leonard, who was carrying our favorite pasta bowl, the one with tomatoes painted all over it.

It twisted my insides, seeing that bowl in his hands. Up until now, every single thing in this house had belonged to me and my mom. But from this day forward, it would belong to Leonard and his Mini-Me, too.

It wouldn't be so bad if I could figure out what my mom saw in Leonard, but I honestly one hundred percent truthfully could not. My mom is gorgeous, even if she has crow's-feet around her eyes that get deeper with every passing year and even if she needs serious help with her wardrobe. She is *statuesque,* which is a fancy word I learned in my fashion magazines for "tall." She has long red hair and, so far, no gray. She has high cheekbones and big green eyes. No wonder she was promoted to news anchor from reporter all those years ago; sure, she's a serious journalist, but she's also "easy on the eyes," as her hair-and-makeup guy, Geoffrey, likes to say.

Leonard, on the other hand, is just a grown-up version of his weird-looking son, with the same ears and the same hair, only better styled. And while I wouldn't call him short, he isn't tall like my dad—maybe five feet ten, tops, which is practically the same as my mom. He is also scrawny; the guy has clearly never lifted weights in his life. My dad, on the other hand, works out all the time, so he has a lot of muscular definition, and his clothes fit him perfectly. And he's always been a very sharp dresser, whereas I'm willing to bet Leonard shops in one midrange store and buys two of everything he likes in different colors. He obviously doesn't put much thought into it. Also he wears pants that show off his MPAL (Male Pattern Ass Loss, a tragic and devastating syndrome common in aging men that I read about in one of my magazines).

I asked my mom bluntly last week what she saw in him. Her face lit up and she said, "He's so smart. And so kind. And he makes me laugh like no one else."

"So? Don't you want to be attracted to him, too?"

"Oh, I am. He's gorgeous. I could get lost in those big brown eyes. And his smile . . . and those lips . . ." I didn't like where this was going and raised my hand to stop her, but not before she said, "I find him incredibly sexy."

"Ewww! Enough!" I shouted.

Clearly my mother is delusional. Leonard is a huge step down. In fact, as far as I can tell, the only thing he has over my dad is that he is *not gay*—which I guess is a biggie, but still. There are a lot of *not gay* men out there, so why on earth did my mom go for this one?

"Isn't this nice?" Leonard said as he sat down across from my mom. His upper lip looked a bit moist, and I realized he was nervous. "Our first meal as a family."

We will never be a family! I shouted, but only in my head because I really wanted that H&M skirt.

Mom served the pasta and Leonard passed around the salad. No one spoke because it was all so incredibly weird. I was about to pick up my fork when the freakazoid spoke.

"Before we begin," he said, "there's a little something my mom used to do at mealtimes."

His mom. I knew what had happened to her, of course. I'll admit I felt a twinge of sympathy for him when he said that.

"What was that?" Mom asked.

"Hold hands with the people on either side of you," he said. I gave my mom a look like, *You have got to be kidding me.* But she held her hand out toward me, and so did Leonard.

Think of the skirt, I told myself. I took their hands, and so did Spewart. Then he and his dad took a deep breath and said, "Truly thankful."

That was it. Talk about corny, no offense to his dead mother. But get this, Mom looked like she had tears in her eyes! "That was beautiful, Stewart. If it's all right with you, I think we should carry on your mom's tradition."

"Thank you, Caroline," he replied. "I'd like that very much."

Barf!

The three of them chatted throughout the meal. I ate in silence, chewing each mouthful carefully because I'd read in one of my magazines that it's a good way to avoid overeating. Stewart, on the other hand, wolfed down his food and filled his plate again. For a midget, he has a huge appetite. "This is delicious," he said, which was a total butt-kiss because the pasta was just so-so.

"Ashley, how do you like your high school?" Leonard asked me in a lame attempt to bring me into the conversation.

I shrugged. "It's fine. It's a school." At least I could be thankful that the egghead wouldn't be going there.

"Stewart's feeling a little nervous, that's all," Leonard said.

"Why? He goes to that school for nerds on the North Shore."

"It's not for nerds," the freakazoid said. "It's for gifteds."

Same diff.

"Actually," Leonard said, "Stewart's decided to transfer."

I dropped my fork with a clatter.

"I feel it would be better for me for a plethora of reasons," Stewart said. Yes, he really said *plethora*. What kid says *plethora*? And what does *plethora* even mean? "I don't want to spend hours every day traveling to and from school. And I thought it would help nurture our new brother-sister relationship if I went to the same—"

That's when I screamed. I'm a good screamer; it's so piercing that my friends tell me I could star in a horror movie. Spewart clapped his hands over his ears.

I ran out of the dining room and into the family room, hoping my mom would follow me. I was going to hurl myself from a running position onto the couch and sob into the cushions. But there was this *super-gross* purple-and-green chair in the way. I had to squeeze past it, which slowed me down, which meant I couldn't hurl myself from a running position anymore.

And there was more. I suddenly became aware that I was surrounded by dozens of hideous ceramic creatures, gazing at me from every corner of the room. They were on the mantelpiece, on the windowsills, on our end tables. Gnomes, fairies, bunnies, dragons, unicorns . . . It was *so not us*!

It was like being in my own private horror movie. It was my house, yet it wasn't my house. It was my life, yet it wasn't my life.

I screamed again. Then I ran upstairs and threw myself on the bed instead, slamming my door behind me.

STEWART

I USED TO WATCH reruns after school of an old seventies sitcom called *The Brady Bunch*. It was about a blended family. The mom had three girls and the dad had three boys, and they had a cheerful housekeeper named Alice. Sure, they had their ups and downs, but overall, practically from the very beginning, everyone got along.

After the whole screaming episode at dinner, I have had to admit that things might not go as smoothly for me and Ashley as they did for Marcia and Greg and Jan and Peter and Cindy and Bobby.

As we cleared the dishes, Caroline kept apologizing. "It's a tough transition for everyone, I know," she said. "And Ashley—well, she's a lot like me when I was her age. I love her dearly, but she's a bit of a drama queen."

"You were a drama queen?" Dad asked, sounding genuinely surprised.

Caroline laughed. "Oh, boy, was I ever. My poor parents. I was an angel—until my twelfth birthday. Then I turned into a demon seed for about five years."

"Well"—Dad smiled—"I'm glad I didn't meet you then."

I did a quick calculation. Ashley was fourteen, so if she followed in her mom's footsteps, she had a good three years of demon seed left.

My heart sank.

I think Dad could guess what was going on in my head because he suggested we take a walk, just the two of us. We went for walks all the time on the North Shore, and I was happy to do something familiar.

It was raining, typical for October, but it was light enough that we didn't need an umbrella. We walked east toward Main on the tree-lined street, past a mix of old and modern homes. I could see people through some of the lit-up windows, other families living their lives.

"I guess it's unrealistic for us to expect Ashley to be happy that we've moved in right off the bat," Dad said to me as we walked along in the almost-dark. "She's had a lot of upheaval in her life."

The sucky part of me wanted to say, *She's had upheaval? She didn't have to change houses, and bedrooms, and neighborhoods! And sure, her parents are divorced, but at least they are both still ALIVE!*

Instead, I nodded and said, "I understand, Dad. Time heals all wounds. . . ."

"And time wounds all heels," we said in unison. Then we

laughed quite a bit, even though we've said this to each other a thousand times. Some jokes really never do get old.

"I guess we're just going to have to give her time to get used to this, and to us," Dad said.

"It'll happen," I said, with more confidence than I felt.

"Of course it will. Who couldn't like us?" He took my hand in the dark and gripped it hard, and even though I am thirteen, I gripped his hand right back.

WHEN WE GOT BACK to the house, Caroline gave me an enormous bowl of cookie dough ice cream, and the three of us watched *Iron Chef* together in the family room. I sat in Mom's chair, and Dad squeezed in with me and ruffled my hair a lot. Caroline sat on the couch, her head resting against the afghan. Like clockwork, Dad and I peeled our socks off and tossed them on the coffee table.

"So," Caroline said during a commercial, "that chair. It's big. And this blanket is very . . . colorful." She was fingering the strands of yellow, orange, blue, and red wool.

"It is, isn't it? Mom loved bright things," I replied.

When *Iron Chef* was done, I went up to my new room. There was still a lot to unpack, but we'd managed to set up my bed and hang up my photos and my posters. Bill Nye the Science Guy smiled down at me over my desk. The solar system was by the door. My favorite poster had pride of place over my bed. Mom had given it to me three years before; it was a cartoon drawing of a human heart, and the heart was saying, "Aorta tell you I think you're awesome."

I let Schrödinger out of the bathroom. I could tell he was

feeling a little freaked out by all the newness, just like I was. I pulled him onto my lap and petted his gray-and-white fur, and soon he started to purr.

When I saw Schrödinger at the shelter, it was love at first sight. His face had a pushed-in look and a chunk of one of his ears was missing. No one knows what happened; he'd been found under a porch with his siblings when he was just two weeks old, and the ear was already gone. He was the runt of the litter, half the size of his brothers and sisters, and very shy, so, animal-behaviorally speaking, it is quite possible that one of his siblings bit off his ear.

Maybe because he looked as vulnerable as I felt, I knew he was the kitten for me. He is a purr machine, and he thinks I'm the greatest person in the whole wide world. My best friend, Alistair, says that's only because I feed him, but I know it goes deeper than that.

"Tomorrow I can let you check out the rest of the house," I told him. "But first you need to get used to this room." I nuzzled my face in his fur. "I need to get used to it, too," I added in a whisper.

I got into my pajamas and crawled into bed, pulling the other afghan on top of me. Schrödinger lay down right by my head, just like he'd done at home.

I mean, the place where I used to live until today.

"This is home now, Schrödinger," I said to him. "We'll love it here, too." Then I repeated it, as if it would help make it true. "We'll love it here, too."

ASHLEY

I WAS SITTING IN my room and kind of regretting that I'd run upstairs and slammed the door. Now I could hardly go back down and watch *America's Next Top Model,* which is only my favorite show of the week. If I did, it would be sending a message that I had cooled down, and I had not.

So I wasn't surprised when Mom knocked a few minutes later. I'd been pretty sure she would. Before I answered I dashed into my bathroom and dabbed my face with water to make it look like I'd been crying. Then I flung open the door.

But it wasn't Mom. It was Leonard.

"Hey, Ashley," he said, his voice all tight and nervous.

"I asked your mom if I could come up and talk to you. I just wanted to say I know this must be really hard on you, and I realize it's going to take time for us to get to know each other. But if you ever need to talk—"

For the second time in one night I slammed my door.

STEWART

WHEN I WAS FOUR years old, I asked my parents one morning over breakfast, "What does *convicted of road rage* mean?"

Dad almost choked on his oatmeal. He showed Mom a headline on the newspaper he was reading: MAN CONVICTED OF ROAD RAGE.

On my fifth birthday, my parents gave me a Lego police car. They watched as I built it without using the instructions. When I was six, I could add up columns of numbers just by looking at them. I liked to take Mom's grocery bills, fold over the total on each so I couldn't see it, and then add the items up in my head.

When I was seven, Mom took me to see a nice lady who did a whole pile of tests. She told my parents I was gifted.

My parents shared what she'd said, and I got very excited for a moment because I honestly thought being gifted involved getting gifts.

"The gift is your mind," my mom told me, which was a huge letdown at first. Still, my parents, Mom especially, seemed pretty pleased. Possibly even relieved. I think it explained a lot. Because being gifted can also mean that you excel in some areas while you stink in others. In my case, even though I scored well above average in intellectual skills, I scored well *below* average in social skills.

And this made a lot of sense.

Because socially speaking, I wasn't doing well at school. I didn't have many friends. The only birthday parties I went to were the ones where the whole class was invited. Looking back, I can see I wasn't being stimulated enough, and when I got bored, I would start to bark like a dog, or crawl under the desks, or eat chalk. (By the way, chalk tastes exactly like you would expect it to: chalky.)

So I already had a reputation as a weirdo, and it only got worse when Freddy Nguyen discovered my secret. Except I didn't know it should be a secret until it was too late.

We always had to go to the bathroom in pairs, and Freddy was partnered up with me one day. I thought I'd locked the stall door, but I clearly hadn't, because suddenly the door swung open and Freddy was staring at me, puzzled. "Is that a *diaper*?"

I didn't feel embarrassed. After all, there was a perfectly rational, scientific reason. "I have an immature bladder. It means my bladder doesn't always signal when I need to go. It's because I was a preemie. I was born six weeks early. The doctor says I'll grow out of it."

The next day, every single kid in my second-grade class started calling me "Poo-art." Not only was it hurtful, it was inaccurate. An immature bladder has nothing to do with excrement. "Poo comes from the colon, not the bladder," I tried to explain to them. "My colon isn't immature!" Those details—even though they were grounded in biological fact—did not seem to matter.

Mom knew I wasn't fitting in very well, and now, armed with my test results, she had the ammunition she needed. She got me into a smaller school that was specifically designed for gifted kids and went all the way up to twelfth grade.

I loved it. I had friends there, like Alistair, who couldn't care less about my immature bladder (which I outgrew a long time ago, thank you very much).

So when we moved away from North Vancouver only six weeks after the school year started, I had a big decision to make: Stay at Little Genius Academy and commute at least two hours every day, or take the plunge and go to the local high school.

Dad told me he would support my decision, no matter what.

About a week before we moved, I said to him over a mac-and-cheese supper, "I think it's time for me to work on my *un*gifted parts."

"What do you mean?"

"The world's a big place. I'm going to have to get along with all sorts of different people, not just people who are more or less like me. So I think I'll try the regular high school."

My dad put down his fork. His eyes watered a little.

"Stewart," he said, "that takes a lot of courage. Your mom would be proud."

"Yes," I replied. "I think she would."

You see, my mom believed that every single person can improve him- or herself. So even though the scientific part of my brain tells me she probably isn't looking down on me from heaven, and that all that is left of her are random molecules, I feel a deep need to do this *for her*. After all, she helped me find a place where I was accepted and where I could thrive. She gave me that solid base. And now that I have it, maybe I need to build on it, and work on the stuff that doesn't come so easily to me. I've even made a list:

TO DO AT NEW SCHOOL

1) Join at least one club. Get involved!

2) Talk to people. Be bold. Make the first move.

3) Read the paper so you can be up on your current events and have interesting things to talk about.

4) Work on your repertoire of jokes—nothing breaks the ice like a good joke.

5) Smile.

6) Try not to make those grunting sounds you've been told you make when you get bored or stressed.

7) Don't get discouraged if following the first six rules doesn't yield big results right away.

I reread my list this morning as I ran a comb through my hair and slapped on an extra layer of deodorant. I held on to a sliver of hope that Ashley might walk to school with me, maybe even introduce me to some of her friends. But when I got downstairs, Caroline said, "Sorry, Stewart. Ashley's already left." Both she and Dad were dressed for work and drinking coffee.

"Thank goodness," my dad said, "because *I* really wanted to walk with you, and now I can!"

It is for reasons like this that I love my dad.

"You look handsome today," Caroline said as she handed me a glass of orange juice. I was wearing jeans and a white button-up shirt and a tie with yellow smiley faces on it, because I hoped it might make me look approachable.

"Thank you."

The microwave dinged and Caroline took out a bowl of porridge. She put it in front of me with a wink. "A little bird told me this was your favorite breakfast."

I didn't have the heart to tell her that my mom always made her porridge from scratch, that she would never have used instant. I just smiled and ate.

Then Dad walked with me to Borden Secondary, which is only five blocks from our new house. We had driven past a couple of times, so I knew it was ten times bigger than Little Genius Academy, but when we arrived on foot, my bowels twisted into knots.

"I need to go back home," I said to Dad. "It's urgent."

Dad understood then, because I never poop in public bathrooms. It is just one of those things I am particular about. So we walked back home at a good clip.

"Back already?" asked Caroline as I tore up the stairs, clutching my stomach. I have never been so grateful for my own bathroom.

Luckily, we'd given ourselves a lot of time, so we were still at school well before the first bell rang. Dad came in with me because we had an appointment with the school counselor. Over the entrance, engraved in the stone, were the words BORDEN SECONDARY SCHOOL, EST. 1927.

The first thing I noticed when we walked through the front doors was the noise. The halls were filled with teenagers, and most of them towered over me. The second thing I noticed was the aroma. It smelled like a mixture of BO and French fries. I cannot tell a lie. I felt terrified.

We found the counselor's office. Her name is Ms. Woodbridge, but she insisted we call her Sylvia. She has a nice smile and very red lipstick. She had seen my school records from Little Genius Academy.

"Based on your academic performance, I've bumped you into ninth-grade courses, to keep you intellectually stimulated," she said. "Unfortunately, it means I've had to put you into ninth-grade phys ed as well because it's the only way I could make the schedule work."

"That's okay," I said.

It was a quick meeting; I got the sense she was a very busy lady. "If you have any problems, or if you just need to talk," she said as she led us back out into the hallway, "my door is always open."

Then she went back inside and closed the door, which I found kind of ironic.

"Do you want me to walk you to your first class?" Dad

asked. Even though he was using his cheerful voice, I could see the little creases of worry in his forehead.

"No, I'm okay." I looked at my schedule. "It should be just down the hall."

"Call me at work when you get home," he said. "I want to hear all about your first day."

"I will." I shook his hand. Then I started the long walk down the corridor toward Room 203. When I reached the door, I looked back. Dad was still standing there. I gave him a little wave. Then I took a deep breath and walked into the room.

At Little Genius Academy, we never had more than twenty students per class. I did a quick tally and counted thirty-three kids.

One of them was Ashley.

ASHLEY

WHEN I SAW THE midget freakazoid walk into my class-room, I honestly thought he was lost. I was at my desk and Lauren was sitting beside me, telling me about her weekend.

"So Claudia texted Amira, then Amira texted Lindsay, who texted Yoko, who texted me, and we all met up down-town on Saturday night to see a movie."

"How come you didn't text *me*?" I asked.

She got all shifty-eyed. "Oh. Well. I thought you'd be busy. With your new, you know, brother." She gave me a smug little grin.

"Lauren, if you call him my brother one more time, I'll tell everyone you stuff your bra."

That wiped the smile off her face.

Claudia described Lauren best when she said to me last

year, "Lauren is like the poor man's version of you." I didn't understand what she meant, till she continued. "You know, not quite as pretty, not quite as well-dressed, not quite as popular."

If I am being totally one hundred percent honest, I would have to say that Claudia hit the snail on the head. My eyes are set perfectly apart; Lauren's are set just a tad too close together. Mine are a piercing blue; hers are mud-brown. My lips are naturally plump; hers are thin. Even though we both have long hair, mine is luxuriant and thick and chestnut brown, while hers is sandy and fine with split ends. I'm just a little bit taller, and a little bit thinner, so clothes hang better on me. Which is fair, since I'm the true *fashionista*—Lauren just buys what I buy (but never in the same color, because I totally forbid it).

It's these small differences that have made her such a good best friend over the years. First of all, she thinks I'm awesome. She always agrees with me. And from my perspective, being around her always makes me feel good about myself, because I'm always just a little bit better than her.

But lately, she's been testing our friendship. Talking back a bit more. Saying things that are kind of mean.

"Well, sure," Claudia said when I mentioned this to her one day at our lockers. "You're like Dr. Frankenstein. You made her in your image. And we all know how that story ends."

Actually, I had no idea. Books have never been my favorite.

"The creature becomes a murderous monster and ruins Dr. Frankenstein's life," Claudia said when she saw the blank look on my face.

"I hardly think Lauren's going to murder anyone," I told her. Claudia can be very dramatic.

"God, you're literal," she replied.

"Not really," I said. "I don't even like reading."

"Not *literate*. *Literal*," she said, rolling her eyes.

That's another reason why I can only be off-and-on friends with Claudia. Half the time she says the smartest things. And half the time I have no idea what she's talking about.

"GUESS WHO WAS THERE?" Lauren said as the class started to fill up with kids.

My mind was drifting a bit as I checked out some of my classmates. I counted three cases of bedhead, one stained shirt, and two severe cases of eye snot. *Honestly, am I the only one who puts any time into personal grooming in the mornings?* I thought. Out loud, I said, "Who?"

"Guess."

Lauren loves to do this. It makes me crazy. "No."

"Jared!"

I tried really, really hard not to react. But it wasn't easy. Jared is only the hottest guy at our school. He transferred from St. Patrick's, a private school, this year. Rumor has it he was kicked out, which makes him even more intriguing; according to this article I read in one of my magazines, women like a hint of mystery and possibly danger in their men. Jared's athletic and tall and broad-shouldered and gorgeous, with wavy black hair and brooding brown eyes. And also, unlike most of the kids at this school, he cares about his appearance. He smiles at me when we pass each other in the halls, but I can't tell if it's a casual smile, as in "I smile at everyone," or a more serious smile, as in "I'd like to get to know you better."

I tried to sound uninterested when I said, "Oh, yeah?"

"Yeah, and he was with some of his friends from his old school, and we all wound up seeing the same movie. And guess what, he sat right behind me and he kept blowing into my hair with his straw." She giggled.

"I hope you didn't giggle like that when he did it," I replied with an air of concern. "We've talked about your giggle. It can make you sound awfully needy."

Lauren's face fell. And for a fraction of a second, I felt better than I had all morning.

But then I heard that voice. "Hi, Ashley," it said, and when I looked up, I saw the nerd-bot in the doorway of *my* English class. And he started to make a beeline toward *me*. In a smiley-face tie!! Cue the horror movie music!!

I shot up from my desk and intercepted him. "What are you doing in here? This is ninth-grade English!"

"They bumped me up a year because I'm gifted."

Oh. My. GOD!

My head was spinning. *This cannot be happening. This is a bad dream and I'm about to wake up.* "Get away from me," I whispered. "Now."

He started blinking a lot. His face went all splotchy and red. Then he scurried to the other side of the room.

I walked back to my desk. Lauren's eyes were wide. "No way," she said. "Nowaynowaynowaynoway. Is that *him*?"

"Shut up, Lauren."

And she did.

But I knew her silence wouldn't last. I knew word would leak out by lunchtime that this hideous creature was living in my house. And I knew who would be responsible for the leak.

But I also knew that by lunchtime, everyone would *also* know that the person responsible for the leak—the person who claims to be a 34C—is really a 32AA.

STEWART

IF I DREW A graph of my first day at Borden Secondary School, it would look like this:

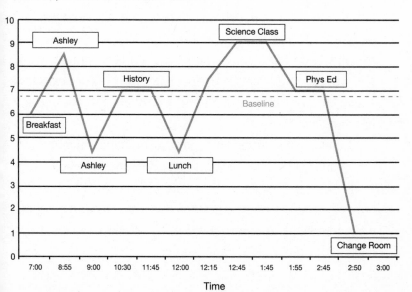

At the beginning of the day, I felt terrified, hence the dip well below my normal mood, which is the baseline. The spike at 8:55 a.m. indicates the brief moment of happiness I experienced when I saw my almost-sister, Ashley, in English class. This is followed immediately by a sharp plunge, when I was reminded that even though she has made no effort whatsoever to get to know me, she hates my guts.

Period 2—history—was uneventful. But lunchtime was a low point. When I walked into the cafeteria with the money Dad had given me as a treat for my first day, it was full of kids from eighth grade up to twelfth, and it was noisy and overwhelming. As I approached the food line, a tall guy with an actual *mustache* turned around suddenly and whacked me in the head with his tray, spilling some of the gravy from his fries on my shirt. "Sorry, kid, I didn't see you," he said.

I believe he was sincere, but he was also huge. And that made me think about a Stephen King novel I'd read called *Under the Dome,* where people in this town find themselves living under an impenetrable bubble one day, and, well, I don't want to give away the ending, but let's just say I started to feel like an ant among giants. So I left the cafeteria without any food and hid under a stairwell until my next class began. It calmed me down, and it brought me back to my baseline.

I had science after lunch, and we're doing chemistry experiments, one of my favorite activities in the whole wide world. I got paired up with a cute girl named Phoebe, but only because her regular partner was home sick. And guess what, she laughed at my joke! I said, "What is the chemical formula for the molecules in candy?"

"I don't know," she replied.

"Carbon-Holmium-Cobalt-Lanthanum-Tellurium." She looked at me blankly till I wrote down the elements' symbols on the front of my notebook. "CHoCoLaTe!"

It's true that she only laughed a little bit. And it's true that she said, "You're an odd duck." But she didn't say it in a mean voice. She said it with a smile. So, as is clear on my chart, that part of the day was a highlight.

My last class was phys ed, and because it was a nice day, the teacher, Mr. Stellar, took us outside to play baseball. I was picked last, which didn't bother me, since after all I am (1) the new guy and (2) shorter than everyone else. Also, (3) my hand-eye coordination is not a strong point, so I struck out when I got to bat. That part of my chart stays around my baseline because at least there were no surprises.

But in the change room afterward, I had what was easily the worst part of my day. Because that was when Mr. Stellar said, "All right, boys, shower time. And I *will* be checking on your way out."

At Little Genius Academy, the school was so small it didn't have showers in its change rooms. So they just scheduled PE for the end of the day. That way our teachers didn't have to put up with a class full of stinky kids, and, if we felt so inspired, we could shower when we got home. (I usually didn't, unless my mom insisted.)

But here at Borden Secondary, it's a whole new ball of wax, as my mom used to say. The moment we got into the change room, boys who were twice my size started to get naked. And when I say *twice my size,* I mean *in all areas.* I didn't know what to do. I just sat quietly on one of the benches and tried not to stare, but it was impossible not to notice that almost every single guy in my class was well into puberty. They had hair in all the right places, and their you-know-whats actually *dangled*.

Mine does not dangle. Mine is more like a protruding belly button. Dad has told me I have nothing to worry about; he says that he, too, was a late bloomer, and that I just need to give it time.

But time was not on my side as I sat in that change room surrounded by naked, hairy guys. I held my street clothes close to my chest and tried to think. At Little Genius Academy, I prided myself on being good at analyzing situations and working out creative solutions. I was on the Model United Nations team last year, representing Denmark, and we had to resolve a food-shortage crisis in a war-torn African country, and I got a perfect score. But solving world hunger was a cakewalk compared to figuring out how not to get naked in front of all these almost-men.

I was stumped. Around me I could hear the guys cracking jokes and talking about a girl named Lauren. "She's only a thirty-two double A," someone was saying. "I heard from a reliable source. She stuffs her bra."

"She's still cute," another boy said.

"Lauren's okay," said a tall, muscular guy. "But you know who's really hot? Ashley Anderson."

"Pretty stuck-up, though," said someone else.

Agreed, I thought, but even though I was somewhat curious, I tried to block out their chatter and concentrate on the issue at hand.

Then I remembered the bathroom stalls. Of course! I got

up and made a dash for them, my clothes still clutched to my chest. I was thinking I could change in there and then wet my hair in the sink so Stellar would think I'd showered.

But just as I got to the stalls, one of the big guys—the one who'd said Ashley was hot—stepped in front of me, blocking my path. He was about to go for his shower, and he was naked except for a towel tied around his waist. Another guy, not as tall, stepped up beside him. "Where do you think you're going?" asked the tall guy.

"To the bathroom," I said.

"You haven't showered. Showers are mandatory."

"I need to pee first."

"Then leave your street clothes out here. I'll hold them for you."

"That's okay."

"I insist." He tried to grab my clothes. I held on tight. "I—I can't have a shower. I don't have a towel."

He looked me up and down. "How old are you, anyway? Eight?" His friend laughed.

"I'm thirteen," I said, offended. I may be short for my age, but I'm not *that* short. "They bumped me up a grade because I'm gifted."

The tall guy smirked. And I suddenly remembered Dad telling me I shouldn't trumpet the fact that I am gifted, because people might think I was bragging.

I think the tall guy thought I was bragging, because he glanced at his friend, then back at me and said, "Gifted, huh?"

I nodded. My head came up to just past his nipples, so I had to look way up.

"You don't seem very gifted at basic personal hygiene, like showering. Maybe you need a little help getting undressed."

"No. Thanks anyway. If you'll excuse me—"

Without warning, he grabbed my gym shorts and yanked them down around my ankles. Luckily I was wearing my favorite boxer shorts underneath.

The tall guy started laughing. "Holy crap! Look!" His friend started laughing, too.

My boxers have cats' faces all over them. My dad bought them for me last Christmas. I don't think they're that funny, but then I remembered a technique I'd learned in Model UN: *Attempt to diffuse a situation by establishing a bond.*

So I started laughing, too. "Yeah, they are pretty goofy," I said, and I actually thought my tactic was working, because we made direct eye contact, and he was still laughing.

Then suddenly he grabbed hold of my boxers and I realized with sphincter-tightening horror that he was about to pull them down, too.

"C'mon, boys, hurry it up in there!" Mr. Stellar shouted as he flung open the door. The tall guy dropped his hands and took a step back. "Jared, tryouts start in five. You'd better get a move on."

"Yes, sir," replied the tall guy. He sauntered away from me toward the showers. I scurried into the stall, locked the door, and changed. When I was done, I wet my hair in the sink. It was enough to fool Mr. Stellar.

But I know I can't keep fooling him. And I certainly can't keep fooling the guy named Jared.

The way I see it, I have a choice to make before next gym

class: either I transfer back to Little Genius Academy, or I come up with a plan.

ON MY WAY HOME from school, I pulled out my phone and called Dad at work. He answered right away. "How are things in the newsroom?" I asked.

"Good, fine. I'm just trying to decide which story to lead with. Events in the Middle East, or the latest kerfuffle in Parliament?"

"I'd take a kerfuffle any day."

"All right. Kerfuffle it is." There was a pause, and then he asked, "How was your day?"

"B," I told him. In reality it was more like a C, but I knew C would worry him, and I knew A would sound too good to be true.

"That's great!" I could hear the relief in his voice. "I want details later. We'll be home right after the newscast, okay?"

"Okay."

When I arrived at the house I now had to think of as home, I stood outside on the sidewalk for a moment. I gazed at the light gray stucco exterior. It is a perfectly nice house. But it doesn't have a lot of character. Our old house had character to burn.

I started to feel a little sad, but then I thought about Schrödinger waiting for me, so I walked up the front steps and reached into my pocket for my key.

It wasn't there. Then I remembered I'd used it when Dad and I had raced back home so I could poop, and I'd left it in the house. I rang the bell in case Ashley was home already, but there was no answer.

Then it started to rain. *Really* rain. I headed through the side gate to the backyard, to see if the patio doors were unlocked. They weren't. But as luck would have it, Ashley was there, in the kitchen. I could see her through the window. She was getting herself a snack. I knocked. She didn't even look up. I knocked again.

This time she looked up. She looked right at me, standing there in the rain. But instead of coming to open the door, she stuck her tongue out at me and left the room.

I couldn't believe it. *You're acting like a toddler!* I wanted to shout.

It was pouring by now. I thought about calling my dad and telling on Ashley, but I knew he couldn't leave work, and anyway, I was pretty sure ratting her out wouldn't make her warm to me any sooner.

I was trying to think of innovative ways to break in when I spotted him.

Ashley's dad. He was opening the door to his laneway house.

I dashed across the yard and said hello.

ASHLEY

I'D HAD SUCH A crappy day. I failed a pop quiz in science. And Lauren had left me no choice but to spread the rumor about her bra-stuffing, but then somehow she tried to make it so it was *my* fault, and she wouldn't even talk to me when the bell rang. Plus she got Lindsay, Amira, and Yoko to not talk to me, either.

Maybe these seem like lousy excuses for not letting Stewart in when he knocked, but I don't know, I guess I also thought I should teach him a valuable lesson, which is "Don't forget your key." I didn't notice it was raining. Honest-to-God-hope-to-die-stick-a-beetle-in-my-eye.

And when I went into his room, it wasn't to snoop or anything, like, *who cares* what the little dweeb has in his room. I just wanted to check up on Shopping Cart or whatever his name is, and maybe pet him a little bit. You know, just a cuddle to cheer me up.

But once I was in there, I couldn't help seeing a bunch of stuff. I mean, it was all right in front of my eyes. First thing I saw were the photos. There must have been ten of them, hung in a row along one wall. Some were of him and his mom, others were of his mom and dad, and a few were of all three of them.

I'll admit I was totally one hundred percent shocked that his mom was pretty. She had a cute little pixie haircut and a nice figure. In all the photos, she had a really lovely smile, and you could tell by the look on her face that she thought Stewart was, like, a god or something. I heard one of my mom's friends say once that biology kicks in and clouds a mother's judgment, and obviously that was what happened in this case; she couldn't see that Stewart was one fugly child.

Anyway, it was kind of spooky looking at all those pictures of a dead person, so I started searching for Shopping Cart. I finally found him hiding under the bed. It was the first time I'd seen him up close. You know how they say dog owners start to look like their dogs? Well, I think Stewart looks a bit like his cat. They are both highly unattractive, and the cat has weird ears, just like Stewart. But I didn't want to give the cat a complex or anything, so I reached out to pet him anyway, and you know what happened? The stupid beast scratched me!

That made me feel really sad for some reason. Maybe because it had happened right after Lauren and my other friends ignored me, but it made me feel like everyone was against me, human *and* animal. And then that made me start to wonder if maybe I was a teeny bit responsible, like maybe I'd gone too far telling people about Lauren's bra, because sometimes I do things that feel right and justified in the moment but that hours later don't feel so right after all. And I was just thinking I should text her an apology when I glimpsed something through the window that made me freeze in my tracks.

It was Stewart, sitting on the couch in the laneway house.

Having tea.

With my dad.

STEWART

MR. ANDERSON—OR PHIL, as he told me to call him once I had introduced myself—seems like a very nice man. When I explained my predicament, he sighed. "Oh, dear. That does sound like something my daughter would do. Come on in. I'll try to call her. But I can't promise she'll pick up when she sees my name."

So I stepped into his laneway house. It is a tiny space— like a dollhouse, but for humans. Except Phil is bigger than most humans; he is well over six feet tall. In my opinion, he is too big for such a little house. "Here, sit," he said, indicating the miniature living room that opened onto the miniature kitchen. He took off his coat, revealing an expensive-looking charcoal-gray suit underneath.

I don't really notice appearances all that much, but even

I could see that Phil is good-looking. When Phil and Caroline were a couple, they must have turned heads. My dad is a quality individual, but I don't think he turns heads. It actually made me feel rather happy, because it had to mean that Caroline had fallen in love with the person my dad is on the *inside* as well as on the outside.

While he hung up his coat, I glanced around his mini-house, which didn't take me very long. It was nicely furnished with smaller versions of things, like a love seat instead of a sofa, a tiny end table, a very skinny leather chair, and no kitchen table at all, just two bar stools pulled up to a counter. An abstract painting hung on one wall. But by far the most striking feature was a blue-and-white Trek road bike hanging from hooks on the opposite wall.

"Nice wheels."

"Thanks. I took up road-biking last year."

"I love bicycles. I'm building an electric one with my friend Alistair."

"Really? Is it for a school project?"

"No, just for fun."

"Well, that's pretty cool." He picked up the phone to call Ashley.

"Did you just get home from work?"

He nodded as the phone started to ring.

"You work at an ad agency, right?"

"That's right. I'm the creative director."

"What does that mean?"

"It means I'm in charge of a few other creative types, and together we come up with ideas for various ad campaigns. TV and print."

"Sounds interesting."

"It is, most of the time. We're working on one that's really fun right now, for a credit union." He hung up, shrugging apologetically. "It went to voice mail. I'm afraid I was right. Would you like to wait here till your dad and Caroline get home?"

I looked outside. Mom and I used to make up words for all the different types of rain in Vancouver. There was *mog* (a combination of mist and fog), *strain* (a steady but not heavy rain), and *skyfall* (a torrential downpour). Today's rain landed somewhere between *strain* and *skyfall*. So I said, "Thanks. I will."

"Can I make you a cup of tea?"

I don't like tea. But it was nice that he was offering, so I said, "Sure." I realized I was starving because I hadn't eaten any lunch. "If you have any snacks, I wouldn't say no." I sat on the love seat while he went to the kitchen and filled the kettle with water.

"Caroline's told me a lot about you," he said. "And I've met your dad a few times."

"Was it weird, meeting my dad?"

"How do you mean?"

"Knowing that he was going to be living in what used to be your house. Sleeping in what used to be your bedroom. Probably on your side of the bed."

He raised an eyebrow. "You really cut to the chase, don't you? Yes, I suppose it was a bit weird. But I'm glad Caroline's happy. And I like your dad. I'd met him at Christmas parties over the years. I met your mom once or twice, too. I was sorry to hear of her passing."

"She didn't *pass*," I said. "She died."

"Right." Phil looked down at the floor, then up at me. "The word *pass* has become all the rage, hasn't it? It's like people don't want to think about death at all, so they won't even say the word. I'm sorry your mom died."

It was the moment that cemented it for me: I liked this guy.

"You must miss her a lot," he continued.

I felt my eyes misting over, but luckily the kettle started to whistle so Phil wasn't looking at me. *I miss her every day,* I said, but only in my head. Out loud I said, "Yes, I do."

He poured the water into the teapot and started rummaging in the cupboards. "Is it weird for *you*?" he asked as he found a sleeve of cookies. "I imagine you must have mixed feelings, moving into a new house that comes complete with new people."

I hesitated. "It's kind of like what you said about Caroline. I'm mostly just happy for my dad. He was sad for a long time."

Phil brought the teapot and some mugs to the living room, a total of three steps. He put them on the little end table, along with a plate of chocolate-covered Digestive biscuits. "So," he said as he sat in the skinny leather chair, "how's Ashley been through all of this?"

"I don't know her very well yet," I replied, picking up three cookies. "But she doesn't seem very happy that we've moved in. She seems kind of . . . angry."

Phil poured some tea into our mugs while I put a whole cookie into my mouth. "I think she *is* angry," he said. "All I can say is, try not to take it personally. I'm the one she's mad at."

"Because you decided to be gay?"

His tea must have been too hot because he almost spit out his first sip. "Let's back up a little, okay? I didn't *decide* to be gay. It's not something you choose."

"That's what my teacher at Little Genius Academy said, too," I replied. "We took a health class, and Mr. Moore said people are *born* with their sexuality."

"Your teacher was right—"

"But what I'm trying to figure out is, if you're born gay, why did *you* only realize it two years ago?"

He nodded. "Ah. I get where you're going with this." He put down his tea. "To quote Lady Gaga, I *was* born this way."

"Then why were you married to Caroline for all those years? Did she know you were gay?"

"No, she didn't."

I stuffed another cookie into my mouth. "So you lied to her," I said with my mouth full.

"Well, yes. I suppose I did. But it wasn't on purpose. I was lying to myself, too."

"Why?"

"Because I didn't want to be gay. I grew up in a very conservative and strict religious family. . . . Maybe it will sound strange, but I made myself believe I was straight. I just wanted a normal life. I wanted a family, kids. . . ."

"Gay people have kids. A girl at my old school has two dads."

"Yes. But I grew up in a small town where that was non-existent. It just seemed like life would be so much easier if I played it straight. No pun intended."

"Poor you." Then I added, "Poor Caroline."

He looked a bit offended. "I know this might be hard to believe, but Caroline and I had a great marriage for the most part. My love for her was very real. It still is."

"Was she surprised when you told her?"

"At first, yes. But then . . . not really. Maybe she knew deep down."

"And Ashley?"

He sighed. "Ashley was devastated. She still hasn't forgiven me."

"For being gay? Or for splitting up the family?"

"Both, I suspect. I think mostly the latter."

"But it's been way over a year."

"Ashley is very good at holding a grudge." He smiled. "Not that I blame her. We were very, very close. . . . She feels betrayed, like I was lying to her, too."

"Well. You kind of were."

"Yes. I kind of was."

I stuffed another cookie into my mouth. "Do you have a boyfriend?"

He had a sip of his tea. "No, I don't. There is someone I'm interested in, a guy in my cycling club. But I have no idea if he's interested in me. . . . To be honest, I have no idea how to do this. I started rather late." He smiled, but he looked kind of sad, and I suddenly got the feeling that he was very lonely.

"Do you know Alan Turing?" I asked.

"Sure. The British fellow who broke the Germans' Enigma code in World War Two. Changed the course of the war."

"Yet in spite of everything he'd done for his country, they

charged him with gross indecency later on. Just because he was gay. He committed suicide by eating a cyanide-laced apple."

Phil cleared his throat. "And you're telling me this why?"

"Because maybe you need to look on the bright side. It has to be easier for you today than it was for Alan Turing."

He opened his mouth to respond, but no words came out. At the same time I saw a flash of movement outside his window. It was Ashley; she'd opened the patio doors.

"Well, look at that," Phil said. "She's letting you in."

I stood. "I should go. I need to check on Schrödinger."

"Schrödinger?"

"He's my cat."

Phil started to laugh. "Schrödinger's Cat. Brilliant."

I smiled. "I thought so, too. Thanks for the tea. And sorry for eating all your cookies," I added, belching a little.

Phil and I shook hands. "Not a problem, Stewart. You're fascinating company. Come over anytime."

ASHLEY

ALL THROUGH DINNER I waited for Spewart to rat me out about locking him out of the house. But he didn't. Instead, he asked my mom and Lenny a whole pile of questions about stories he'd seen on the news. It was all "Conservatives this," "Russia that." After a while I just tuned out.

Then he said, "The outfit you wore on air was very nice, Caroline."

"Why, thank you," my mom replied. "I have to give all the credit to Ashley." She turned to me. "I wore the jacket you picked out for me. The mocha one."

I couldn't stop my lips from curling upward into a smile. "I know. I saw."

"You watched the news together?" Mom said. She sounded

so hopeful. I even saw her share a look with Lenny. Like they seriously thought the midget and I might be bonding!

"No," I said. "I just wandered through to see what you were wearing. Making sure you weren't committing any fashion crimes."

"Ashley has a great eye," Mom continued. "She helps me pick out almost everything I wear on air. I'd be lost without her."

"It's true," I agreed, warming to the subject. "She has zero fashion sense."

"I don't think that's true," Lenny said.

But Mom just laughed. "Oh, it's true. Her dad, on the other hand, has impeccable taste in clothes."

"Do you think that's because he's gay?" Stewart asked. "Or am I just perpetuating a stereotype?"

Suddenly I felt like I was underwater. They kept talking, but they sounded like the adults on *Charlie Brown*. *Wah-wah-wah-wah-wah-waah*.

Finally I found my voice. "Who told you my dad's gay?"

They all turned to look at me. Stewart looked puzzled. "What do you mean? He *is* gay."

"Who. Told you."

"I probably did," Leonard said with a shrug.

"And who told *you*?"

"I did, Ashley. Obviously," Mom said.

"Why?"

"Because we're living together. Because when all of this happened, Leonard was the one person I felt I could turn to. Because I love him, and I'm never going to keep secrets from him."

60

I couldn't think of a way to argue with that, so I turned to Leonard instead. "And then you told *him*?" I said, pointing a finger at Stewart. "Why did you think it was any of your business?"

Leonard put down his knife and fork. "We were about to move in with you. Phil lives within spitting distance. Stewart had a lot of questions. I answered his questions as honestly as I could." He looked toward my mom, confused. "I don't understand what the problem is."

"Ashley, it's not like it's a secret—"

"It *is too!*" I wailed. "None of my friends know. None of them!"

Mom looked surprised. "Really? Not even your closest friends? Not even Lauren?"

"*Especially* not Lauren!" *God!* How could I explain to someone who hasn't been a teenager for centuries that best friends are the ones who are most likely to use your darkest secrets against you one day, and stab you right in the back?

"Gee," Stewart said. "I would tell my best friend, Alistair, anything."

"That's 'cause you're a *freak* and everything you do is freaky!" I saw Leonard's jaw tighten; it was the first time I'd seen him look mad.

"Ashley, that was completely uncalled for," Mom started.

"So? This entire situation is completely uncalled for! I didn't ask for these two strangers to move into our house. I didn't ask for you and Dad to divorce. And I didn't ask for Dad to be gay!" I stood up, pushing my chair back so hard it clattered to the floor. Then I put my face inches from

Stewart's. "If you so much as breathe a word to *anyone* at school about my dad, I will have you killed!"

"Okay, that is totally inappropriate," Leonard began.

"Shut up, Leonard."

"Ashley Eleanor Anderson," said Mom. "I have never been so ashamed—"

"Welcome to the club!! I've never been so ashamed, either! I am counting the days till I can become unconstipated!!"

Mom looked puzzled. "What does that have to do with this? Do you need to eat more fiber?"

"No, the other meaning!" I shouted. "The one that means I can divorce my family!"

There was silence for a moment—then the little freakazoid started to laugh. He tried to stop. He put a hand over his mouth. But it was too late. I'd seen him do it.

"I think," he said, "the word you're looking for is *emancipated.*"

I looked at each of them. They were all trying not to laugh. And I felt so angry and so humiliated because words, like a lot of other things, are not my strong point, and I needed all of them, especially Mom, to understand how upset I was. I needed them to see things from my point of view for a change, and instead it was all turning into a big joke.

"I hate you all," I said. Then I walked out.

Mom followed me upstairs. She tried to talk to me using her calm voice. She said she was disappointed in my behavior. She said she was concerned that I hadn't told any of my friends the truth about Dad. She asked if I wanted to go "talk to a professional," like I'm a crazy person. But I was still angry, so I kept shouting, and eventually her calm voice was replaced by her exasperated voice. Just before she left my room, she announced that I wouldn't be getting my allowance this weekend.

There goes the H&M skirt.

STEWART

PERCENTAGE-WISE, I would give the rest of my week an average of 73. What follows is the daily breakdown.

TUESDAY—76%

I didn't have to worry about gym class, because every other day I have French, home ec, math, and business ed. Lucky for me, Jared isn't in any of my Day Two classes. Also lucky for me, Phoebe is in my business education class.

Unlucky for me, Ashley is in my math class.

I may not be the best reader of social cues, but when someone yells, "I hate you all," it is pretty hard to misinterpret.

And as I told Dr. Elizabeth Moscovich on the phone late last night, Ashley still hates her own father a year and a half later, which tells me she's really good at holding a grudge. In fact, I told Dr. Elizabeth Moscovich all the gory details, even though Ashley threatened me with murder, because (1) I know that everything I say to her is protected by a little something called *doctor/patient confidentiality,* and (2) I figured it was good for an outside party to know about the threat, just in case Ashley ever follows through.

To be honest, Dr. Elizabeth Moscovich sounded tired. It was after eleven when I called her. Technically I'm not seeing her anymore, but when we moved, she gave me her home number in case of an emergency, and I felt that being threatened with assassination qualified.

"Try to see it from her perspective," Dr. Elizabeth Moscovich said. "You and your dad were rather abruptly thrust upon her. She must feel like her whole world's been turned upside down."

I confess that I don't like it when Dr. Elizabeth Moscovich takes someone else's side. "What about *my* world?" I asked. "*My* world's been like riding the Hellevator at the fair!"

Dr. Elizabeth Moscovich agreed and said some kind things, which made me feel better. So much better that I told her about Ashley saying she couldn't wait till she became "unconstipated." It made me laugh all over again.

I think Dr. Elizabeth Moscovich wanted to laugh, too, but instead she said, "Now, Stewart, we've talked about this. Not everyone is intellectually gifted like you. Different people are smart in different ways."

Maybe that's true, but I'm beginning to suspect that if you blew into one of Ashley's ears, the breeze would come right out the other side.

For example, after school on Tuesday I went into the family room to watch TV. Ashley was already there, watching some celebrity gossip show. She didn't look happy to see me, but I thought, *Tough. This is my house now, too.* So I sat in the purple-and-green chair and peeled off my socks. Schrödinger wandered in and jumped up onto my lap.

When a commercial came on, she muted the TV and asked, "Why did you give your cat such a dumb name?"

"It's not a dumb name. Schrödinger was a famous physicist. And he developed a thought experiment. . . ." I stopped. "It's actually super-complicated."

"So? You think I won't get it?"

Yes, I thought. But all I said was, "Okay. Do you know about the Copenhagen interpretation of quantum mechanics?"

"The what of the what?"

"It basically says that matter on a microscopic level, like an atom, can be in two places at the same time—that is, until you *observe* the atom. Then it will just be in one place."

Ashley yawned. "That's ridiculous. Nothing can be in two places at once."

"Well, in one sense you're right. Because the theory doesn't work on a macroscopic level, meaning, everything we can see around us. Like, this chair I'm sitting in can't be in two places at once."

"Thank God for that. One place is bad enough."

"Anyway, Schrödinger wanted to challenge the Copenhagen interpretation. So he came up with this thought experiment. You put a live cat into a box, along with a vial of poison and a radioactive substance. If even one atom of the radioactive stuff decays, a mechanism will trip a device that will break the vial and kill the cat. But before you open the box, you can't know if the cat is dead or alive, and if you subscribe to the Copenhagen theory, then you must believe that the cat is both dead *and* alive at the same time. Which Schrödinger was trying to point out was kind of ridiculous."

Ashley's eyes had grown wide with horror. "That's total animal cruelty! Does PETA know about this?"

I took a deep breath. "I don't think PETA existed back then," I explained patiently. "And it was a *thought* experiment. Meaning, he didn't really do it. He was just trying to point out the discrepancy between matter on a microscopic level and matter in our actual, observable world. It was meant as a discussion piece." I pointed down at Schrödinger. "The experiment is known as Schrödinger's Cat."

She stared at me blankly for a moment. Then her show came back on, and she unmuted the TV. Our conversation was officially over.

WEDNESDAY—61%

On Wednesday after lunch (which I ate under the stairwell), I had science with Phoebe again. It wasn't quite as fun, because her friend and lab partner, a girl named Violet, was back. "What did one quantum physicist say to another quantum physicist when he wanted to fight him?" I whispered to them near the end of class. "Let me atom!"

Phoebe snorted, but Violet just rolled her eyes. I don't think she appreciates my sense of humor.

Then I had phys ed. I am not proud of what I did, but as I had not yet figured out a solution to the Jared Conundrum, my options were limited. So I wrote a note.

Dear Mr. Stellar,

Please excuse Stewart from gym class today. He has a doctor's appointment. It is nothing serious in case you were wondering. Just a wart.

Sincerely, Leonard Inkster

My hand was shaking when I handed the note to Mr. Stellar before class, but he barely even glanced at it. "See you next time," he said.

Then I left school and jogged home just so I could say I'd gotten some exercise.

When Dad and I took our nightly walk, I almost told him about the Jared Conundrum. Since Mom died, we've made a point of trying to tell each other everything. But when I looked at him under the glow of the streetlamps, I just couldn't do it. I knew it would make him sick with worry. I knew he'd get the school involved, or insist I go back to Little Genius Academy. And while it's hard for me to explain, I feel like I need to take care of this on my own, not just for my sake, but for my mom's.

So even though I avoided Jared, I could only give

Wednesday a 61 percent. I had to deduct points for (1) forging my dad's signature and (2) lying.

THURSDAY—74%

An average and uneventful day.

FRIDAY—82%

Today is a professional development day, so no school, which is a stroke of luck. I have three whole days to try to figure out the Jared Conundrum. And while I haven't done much except unpack the rest of my stuff and do homework, I have anticipatory excitement that immediately pushes today over 80 percent.

First, my dad and I are on our own tonight because Caroline is emceeing a fund-raiser/fashion show and she's taking Ashley. We are going to order a pizza and hang up my mom's big painting, *Mother and Child.* Afterward we're going to watch *E.T.,* which is only the best movie of all time.

And second, Alistair is coming over on Saturday and spending the night. It's going to be great. We're going to work on my bike, and later we're going to have an epic game of Stratego.

Best of all, if there's one person who's even better at problem-solving than I am, it's Alistair.

I can get his brain working on the Jared Conundrum, too.

ASHLEY

"WHAT DO YOU MEAN, he's having a sleepover?"
I said to my mom on Saturday morning. She'd insisted
I go with her to a fashion show fund-raiser the night before, saying we needed some "mother-daughter bonding
time." It wound up being really fun, and in fact we bonded
so much that I even asked her sweetly on the way home
if she'd reconsider giving me my allowance. She said no.
That led to another heated argument, and by the time she
pulled up out front, we were crabby at each other all over
again.

And now I had crabbiness on top of crabbiness. *"I'm* having a sleepover!" I protested. Lauren and I have sleepovers
about once a month. We take turns between houses, but
we both know that my house is better, since my bedroom is

bigger, my music's better, my makeup is better, and I have better low-fat snacks.

Mom was making brunch, still in her bathrobe. There was a pile of dirty dishes on the counter with bits of food crusted all over them, left there by Lenny and Squiggy the night before. "All they had to do was rinse them and put them in the dishwasher," Mom muttered to herself. "Is that so hard?"

"Mom! Have you heard a word I've said?"

She sighed. "Yes. I heard you. So you'll both have sleepovers. So what?"

I put my hands on my hips. "I just want to state for the record that I feel like I and my wishes are being seriously taken for granite lately."

"For *granted*," she replied just as the doorbell rang. I followed Mom into the foyer. A dark-skinned but equally geeky-looking version of Stewart stood at the door, a duffel bag in his hands. "Hello, I'm Alistair Singh. You must be Caroline and Ashley. Pleasure to meet you."

"You too, Alistair. Stewart's in his room. You can go on up. It's on the left at the end of the hall."

"Thanks." Alistair slipped off his shoes, then nodded toward the living room. "I see you've found a home for Janice's painting."

"Janice?" I said.

"Stewart's mom," he said before he took off upstairs. Mom and I looked at each other, puzzled. We peered into the living room.

I almost screamed. And totally one hundred percent no joke, my mom almost screamed, too.

A massive oil painting hung over the fireplace. The space had been empty since Dad moved out; he took very little with him, but he did take the painting that used to hang there, because he'd bought it before he and Mom were married. It was an *abstract,* meaning it looked like a kindergarten kid had thrown paint at a canvas.

This thing was not abstract. It was very, very lifelike. And it was unmistakably Stewart's dead mother, breastfeeding her baby. Who was unmistakably Stewart. And the breasts were *bare*!

"Did you know about this?" I asked.

Mom looked pale. "No. I mean, yes—I've seen it at their old house. But no, I didn't realize they'd brought it here. I thought it had gone into storage." She pulled her bathrobe tight, hugging herself. "They must have hung it up last night. I don't know how we missed it when we came in."

"Mom, it can't stay. You know it can't stay! It's practically pornography!"

"Ashley, breastfeeding is perfectly natural—"

"*WhatEVER!* It doesn't mean we should have to look at it twenty-four-seven in our own house!"

Mom was quiet for a moment. Then she said, "It's not to my taste, either. I'll talk to Leonard when he's back from his fencing class."

Yup. Uh-huh. Lenny *fences.* Honestly, I sometimes wonder if, after my dad left and before she started dating *her boss,* my mother had a mini-stroke, something that affected the "who I'll be attracted to" part of her brain. Then again, she married a guy who turned out to be gay, so maybe the "who I'll be attracted to" part of her brain never worked all that well.

Before we'd even left the foyer, the doorbell rang again. It had to be Lauren. "Oh, no," I groaned. "If Lauren sees this painting, I might as well never go back to school ever again."

"Sweetheart, she's your best friend. I don't think you give her enough credit. I'm sure she'll understand, just like she'd understand if you told her about your dad."

I shook my head. Honestly, it's been centuries since my mom was a teenager, so she's totally forgotten about the Social Ladder.

See, I'm pretty much at the top of the Social Ladder in my grade. It wasn't always this way; back in elementary school, we were all the same—kind of dorky, but happy. Then, in the summer before seventh grade, everything changed for me. I got my period and went from being this flat-chested, goofy twelve-year-old to a twelve-year-old with a woman's body. I hated it. I'd walk down the street and guys would stare at me, and not just guys my age, but guys who were my dad's age. It was super-creepy, and I just wanted to go back to being that flat-chested little girl again.

But when seventh grade started, I learned pretty fast that my new look gave me a strange kind of power. It was like both the boys and the girls were a little bit in awe of the new me. So after a while, I did what anyone would do: I used it to my advantage. And practically one hundred percent immediately, I was perched right on top of that ladder.

Lauren is just underneath me, along with Yoko. Amira

and Lindsay are a rung lower, and Claudia is a bit lower still. (People like Stewart don't even count. They don't even have a foot on the ladder. They can't even touch the ladder. They are forbidden to go anywhere *near* the ladder.) Contrary to what I heard my math teacher say one day under his breath, I'm no dummy. I know that the people directly beneath me on the ladder—meaning people like Lauren—would love to see me lose my footing so they can take my place. Which means I can never appear weak or vulnerable, or people like Lauren will go in for the kill.

If I am one hundred percent totally honest, I sometimes long for the olden days, when we were all just little dorks. Things are so much more complicated now.

"I'll take Lauren downtown," I said to my mom, grabbing my cute puffy blue jacket. "Please, I beg of you, make it be gone by the time we get back." I opened the front door. Lauren stood there with her overnight bag. "Let's get out of here. The troll's in his room with his troll friend." I stepped outside.

"Can I just use your bathroom—"

"We'll find one downtown." I grabbed her overnight bag and tossed it into the foyer before slamming the door behind me.

We took the bus to Granville Street and wandered around the Pacific Centre mall. I showed Lauren the skirt I was dying to get at H&M. "I thought you were going to have enough money to get it this weekend," she said.

"Nope, my mom canceled this week's allowance 'cause I was rude to the nerd-bot."

Lauren giggled. "Ugh, who wouldn't be rude to him?

He's such a Tragic!" *Tragic* is our word for super-geeks and super-losers. There is a whole army of Tragics at our school.

I giggled, too, and for the next hour or so, we bonded over ridiculing Stewart and other Tragics in our grade, like Lardy, whose real name is Larry, and Sam, who could be a boy or could be a girl—we honestly have no idea. Then we wandered down Robson Street and went into Forever 21. Lauren tried on pants and I tried on some stuff just for fun.

"You won't believe who talked to me in history yesterday," she said while we were in side-by-side dressing rooms.

"Who?"

"Jared!"

My stomach lurched. Lauren's lucky; she has three classes with Jared. I don't have any.

"What did he want?"

"He was wondering if I knew of any parties this weekend. I had to say no, because I don't. But for a minute I actually thought he was going to ask me out! Then the teacher told us to be quiet."

We stepped out to show each other what we'd tried on. Lauren was wearing a pair of red skinny jeans.

"What do you think?" she asked. "I like them."

"Twirl around," I said. She did. They looked good on her. Really good. But I had to remember the Social Ladder. "They're a great color," I said, "but they kind of make your ass look fat."

She didn't buy the pants. I felt a twinge of guilt. But then I reminded myself: high school is a doggy-dog world.

* * *

75

ON THE BUS BACK home, I texted Mom.

Is it gone?

It felt like it took forever to get her reply.

Yes.

Better still, when we got back, the troll was out with his troll friend. Mom and Leonard were out, too.

"Can I see the cat?" Lauren asked. I'd told her about Shoe Box and how fugly he was.

For the second time in a week, I went into Stewart's room. Shoe Box darted under the bed, and none of Lauren's coaxing would get him to come out.

Then we spotted the thing on his desk.

It was made of spaghetti and marshmallows, and it was huge. Clearly Stewart and his nerd-ball friend had spent the day building it. It looked kind of like the Eiffel Tower.

Lauren and I locked eyes. "Dare you," she whispered.

It was a no-brainer. I picked up Stewart's math book. I held it over the tower.

I let go.

STEWART

ALISTAIR AND I HAD an awesome morning. First, we spent a long time in the basement, working on my bicycle. This is a pet project of mine; a few months ago I bought a used ten-speed for just sixty dollars, and I'm converting it into an electric bike. I'm trying to do the entire conversion for under one hundred dollars, which is a challenge, but doable.

After we'd spent a couple of hours on the motor, we needed to blow off some steam. Caroline let us take a box of spaghetti and a bag of marshmallows from the kitchen, and we built our own version of the Eiffel Tower in my room. When we were done, we decided we should get some fresh air, so we headed downstairs.

We were about halfway down when I heard my dad and

Caroline arguing. I stopped and motioned for Alistair to do the same.

"We didn't mean to upset you," my dad was saying. I could just see him in the living room; he was still wearing his fencing uniform. He looks very good in his fencing uniform—taller somehow, and more muscular.

"I know that. But there are good surprises and not-so-good surprises, and I'm sorry, but this one falls into the latter category."

"What don't you like about it? Is it the artistry? I think you'd agree Janice had a real talent."

"She did, absolutely. But, well—think about Ashley. She's a teenager, Leonard. A very difficult, challenging teenager, but still. The nudity is mortifying to her."

"But it's a perfectly natural—"

"I know, I know—"

"Famous artists have painted mother and child scenarios for centuries. Heck, there are millions of such paintings of the baby Jesus and Mary—"

"But they're not in our house. And this isn't the baby Jesus and Mary. It's very clearly Stewart and his mom."

My dad was quiet for a second. "I think Ashley isn't the only one who's bothered by it."

"Leonard, I love you. And you know I never expect you to forget Janice, nor would I want you to. But I'm not sure how I feel about her gazing down at me, day after day . . . especially with her breasts exposed. . . . I could take the easy way out and blame it solely on Ashley, but you're right. It's not to my taste, either."

I waited for my dad to tell her what the painting means

to me. What it means to him. I waited for him to tell her that we'd hardly brought any of our stuff to her house and maybe she and Ashley could be a little more accommodating.

But he didn't. Instead, he took Caroline in his arms. "I'll talk to Stewart. We'll take it down. Just let me eat breakfast first, will you?"

"I made your favorite. Oatmeal buckwheat pancakes. There aren't many left over, though. Stewart has a voracious appetite." They headed into the kitchen.

"You love that painting," Alistair whispered after they were gone.

I nodded. I realized I was feeling something I don't feel very often, and that is anger. I don't like feeling anger. I avoid it at all costs. So I just said, "Let's go," and the two of us grabbed our jackets and left the house without saying good-bye to anyone.

ALISTAIR AND I WALKED east toward Main Street. I didn't want to talk about the painting, so instead I filled him in on the Jared Conundrum.

"Wow," he said. "That's tough."

"Any ideas?"

He thought for a while. "I know it's a long commute, but . . . maybe you should come back to Little Genius Academy."

This, from the guy who'd won Problem Solver of the Year in our school's Model UN two years in a row. "Really, Alistair? That's all you've got?"

"Sorry," he said. "But Jared sounds like a sociopath. And

79

it's my understanding that sociopaths are hard to deal with on a rational level." He had a point.

"But I made a pact with myself that I'd try to make this work. I made it on behalf of my mom. I can't give up after a week. Can I?"

"I guess not. And now that I think of it, you couldn't come back to Little Genius anyway. Your spot was snatched up by some girl on the waiting list."

Hearing that made my heart sink.

We turned onto Main, which is one of the highlights of being in this neighborhood instead of on the North Shore. It has a real hustle-bustle about it. We headed south, walking past a bunch of one-of-a-kind clothing stores; a butcher shop; Japanese, Thai, and Caribbean restaurants; a Legion hall; a wool shop; five coffee shops; and a thrift store.

We were almost past the thrift store when I noticed Phoebe. She was inside, looking through a rack of clothes with Violet.

"C'mon," I said to Alistair. I pulled him into the store and marched right up to Phoebe. "Hi!"

She glanced up from the rack. "Oh, hey, Stewart," she said. I saw her share a look with Violet.

"This is my friend Alistair. Alistair, meet Phoebe and Violet. They go to my new school."

"Nice to meet you," Phoebe said with a smile. She has a beautiful smile. Her teeth are straight and white. The rest of her face is pretty, too. It is a very symmetrical face, which I find aesthetically pleasing. She has almond-shaped eyes and light brown skin and shoulder-length, jet-black hair. She was wearing jeans and a plain gray T-shirt, which is all I've ever seen her wear (with variations on the T-shirt color); this tells me she doesn't put a lot of thought into her appearance, an admirable quality since there are so many more important and interesting things to think about.

"Looking for anything in particular?" I asked them while Alistair wandered deeper into the store.

"Not really. Once I found the coolest jacket here, so we always have a quick look when we pass by," said Phoebe.

"Can we ask you a question?" Violet asked as she kept flicking through the rack of clothes. She wore a knee-length skirt with black tights and a pair of lime-green Converse high-tops.

"Shoot."

"Is it true you're Ashley Anderson's brother?"

"No, not really. I mean, my dad and I have moved in with her and her mom. But we're not related by blood."

"Thank God for that," Violet muttered.

"What do you mean?" I asked.

"Just that she's a horrible human being and we hate her guts."

"Violet," Phoebe said in a warning voice.

"What? She calls us *Feeble* and *Violent*. Count yourself lucky that you don't share any of her genetic code."

"Her mom and dad are really nice," I said.

"Sorry, Stewart," Phoebe said. "Maybe you know another side to Ashley."

"Not so far, no," I confessed. "But I keep hoping for an improvement in our relationship."

"Yeah, well. Good luck with that," Violet said. She glanced at her watch. "I have to run. I'm supposed to meet Jean-Paul at his house."

"Who's Jean-Paul?" I asked.

"Her boyfriend," Phoebe replied. "He goes to the French immersion high school. I have to run, too. Mandarin lesson. See you Monday." She and Violet left the store.

I looked around for Alistair, spotting him near the back by the EMPLOYEES ONLY sign. He was digging around in a large cardboard box.

"I may have found a solution to your problem," he said. Then he pulled something out of the box and held it up for my inspection. "Not foolproof. But it would offer a certain amount of protection."

I smiled. "Alistair, you still get my vote for Problem Solver of the Year. It's perfect!"

WHEN WE GOT HOME, the weekend kind of went downhill. First of all, the painting had disappeared from the living room, before my dad had even talked to me about it. Second, our Eiffel Tower had been destroyed. Ashley tried to blame it on Schrödinger, but I knew better. I could tell from the trajectory of the broken spaghetti strands that a large, solid object had been dropped on it from above, something like my math book, which wasn't where I'd left it. Third, Ashley and Lauren blasted music all night while Alistair and I tried to play Stratego. I have nothing against loud music, but Ashley and Lauren sang along to every song, and I can say with some authority that they are both tone-deaf.

Fourth, Alistair whipped my butt in Stratego.

Now it's Sunday. Dad tried to talk to me about the painting, after Lauren had left and Alistair had been picked up. He found me snuggling with Schrödinger in my room.

"I'm sorry, buddy. But I had to respect Caroline's wishes."

"What about *my* wishes?"

Dad sighed. "Well, technically speaking, it *is* her house—"

"So we should just feel like guests in it?"

"No, but we have to be able to compromise."

"We *have* compromised. *We* moved. *We* only brought a few things with us. And now one of them is gone."

"Not gone. It's in the basement. If you want, we can hang it in your room instead."

So we carried the painting up to my room. Caroline helped. She was apologetic about not wanting it in the living room, but she also stuck to her guns.

Dad held the painting up against one of my walls. While I looked at it from the other side of the room, the cold, hard truth hit me. I didn't want it hanging in here, either. It is a very large painting. And while I will love my mom for eternity, I don't want to gaze at a baby-me drinking from her bare boobs every time I wake up and every time I do homework and every time I lie down. That's why the living room had seemed so perfect; it was supposed to be something that everyone could enjoy, but on a limited basis.

So we carried the painting back down to the basement. Dad and I agreed that next time we visit the storage locker, we'll bring the painting with us. Caroline suggested we take something else *out* of the storage locker and bring it home, and I was grateful to her for that.

Still. I know that this will sound possibly overly emotional, but every time we get rid of something else that Mom loved, I feel like we're letting a little bit more of her memory die. I feel like we're betraying her, Dad especially.

I want my dad to be able to move on with his life. I want him to be happy with Caroline. But I don't want him to ever forget or stop loving my mom.

ASHLEY

OH. MY. *GOD!!!!*

Can my life just be normal for twenty-four hours without one of my family members ruining everything?? Is that too much to ask??

Lauren and I had a great sleepover. We played music really loud and sang along. We also experimented with makeup. When we were done, we voted on whose makeup job looked best and I won. Then we went on Facebook, and Lauren showed me Jared's home page, because she is "friends" with him. "Did he friend you?" I asked.

"No. I friended him," she replied, which made me feel better.

So I friended him, too, and guess what? He accepted my

friend request after ten seconds! And *then* guess what?? He said *hi* in chat! Lauren and I practically fell off my bed.

After a lot of discussion about what I should say back, I wound up typing *Hey*. But I guess I waited too long, because he didn't type back. He'd gone offline.

But still, he did say *hi,* and that's more than he'd said to Lauren. We scrolled through the photos he'd posted and we each "liked" one of him by a pool taken in the summer. He's wearing a bathing suit and nothing else, and let's just say that if Calvin Klein ever saw that picture, he'd ask Jared to be one of his underwear models.

This morning Mom made French toast, but since Lauren thinks her thighs are too big and I worry about my upper arms, we only had one slice each and a bunch of fruit. Then Lauren said she should go 'cause she had a lot of homework to do. I walked her to the front door. Stewart was saying goodbye to his troll-clone on the sidewalk. Albatross or whatever his name is got into a Lexus driven by a pretty South Asian woman.

Then, just as the Lexus pulled away, a silver MINI Cooper drove up. The driver was a handsome black guy. I'd never seen him before.

But I'd seen the guy in the passenger seat many times. It was my dad.

Things moved in slow motion.

I saw the man in the driver's seat lean toward my dad in the passenger seat, and I suddenly knew what was about to happen.

"Hey, isn't that—" Lauren began.

"Bat in the cave!" I shrieked, turning her toward me and away from the car.

"What?"

"Booger. You've got a booger," I said.

"Oh, gross!" She dug around in her pocket for a Kleenex. While she dealt with the nonexistent booger, the man in the driver's seat kissed my dad.

On the lips.

Stewart saw it, too.

My dad smiled, turned—and spotted me, Stewart, and Lauren. His smile vanished.

Lauren tucked the Kleenex into her pocket. "Gone?" she asked me.

"Gone."

She turned around just as Dad climbed out of the car, carrying an overnight bag. "Who's the guy with your father?"

"A guy he works with. He just came back from a business trip," I lied.

"Hey, guys," my dad said, looking super-uncomfortable, which was only appropriate. The MINI Cooper pulled away.

"Hi, Phil," Stewart said.

"Hi, Mr. Anderson," said Lauren.

I, on the other hand, didn't say a word. I just marched back into the house and slammed the door.

MOM WAS IN HER bedroom, doing a yoga routine to a podcast. She was in warrior two when I told her what I'd seen. I thought she'd be upset. Instead she said, "He told me a few weeks ago that there was someone he was interested in. He met him in his cycling club, I think."

"And you're okay with that?"

"Honestly? It brought up a lot of mixed emotions. But I keep reminding myself that I've moved on—why shouldn't he?"

"But what if one of my friends sees him in public?" Then another, more horrifying thought occurred to me. "What if he starts bringing this guy home??"

Mom stopped doing her yoga routine. She smoothed a piece of hair from my face. "Ashley, I'm truly sorry this is so hard for you. But try to put yourself in your dad's shoes for a moment. Why shouldn't he bring this person home? I brought Leonard home, didn't I?"

"This is different. You know this is different!"

"Why? Because he's gay? You're sounding remarkably homophobic, which is not how we raised you."

"I'm *not*. But some of my friends might be."

"If your friends have a problem with it, then they're clearly not your friends."

"Oh my God. You don't understand anything. Why is everyone in this family so determined to ruin my life?"

Mom sighed. She went back to her yoga, moving into downward dog. "You're right. There's no use pretending anymore. We actually hold secret meetings once a week, just to figure out new ways to torment you and make your life a living hell."

"I *knew* it!"

"That was my attempt at sarcasm, sweetheart. Contrary to what you believe at this stage in your life, we aren't all out to get you. So please stop being so melodramatic."

This made no sense whatsoever. How can you be mellow *and* dramatic at the same time?

STEWART

TODAY WAS WHAT I like to call an Alexander Fleming kind of day.

Fleming was a scientist, and notoriously messy. One day he went on vacation, leaving some bacterial cultures sitting on his desk. When he came back, he found a weird fungus growing on some of his cultures, and the bacteria weren't thriving around the fungus. He thought his experiments were ruined—till he figured out he had just made a little discovery called penicillin. What he thought was going to be a very bad day turned out to be one of his best.

I didn't make any revolutionary scientific discovery, but my day also went much, much better than originally expected.

Phys ed wasn't till last period, so I had a lot of hours to

get through first. My stomach was twisted in knots all day. All I could think about were the communal showers, and the possibly sociopathic Jared.

In English, we got back our essays on *To Kill a Mockingbird,* and I got an A+. I don't know what mark Ashley got, but her face turned beet red when she saw her grade, and she quickly flipped her paper over, so I'm guessing it wasn't good.

Then, when I stopped by my locker at the beginning of lunch, I overheard Violet asking Phoebe if she wanted to go to her house for lunch.

"I can't. I have Mathletes."

"Mathletes?" I asked. I knew I was butting into their private conversation, but I couldn't help it. "This school has Mathletes?"

"Yeah," Phoebe said, shoving her books into her locker.

"I love Mathletes! I was team captain at Little Genius Academy!"

"You should really stop saying your old school's name out loud," Violet said. She and Phoebe started walking down the hall. I followed.

"One of my goals is to join at least one club," I told Phoebe as I kept pace with her. "Do you think I could come?"

Phoebe shrugged. "I don't know. I guess."

So I followed her up the stairs to Room 222. I was surprised that only five kids were there, not including Phoebe and me. Their team was a third the size of the one at Little Genius. The teacher who runs the club, Mr. Fernlund, seemed more than happy to let me sit in. "Please," he said. "We could use another member."

It was fantastic, because (1) I didn't have to eat lunch

under the stairwell, and (2) I love math. We got to work on problems like *There are seven people at a party. Each person shakes hands once with every other person there. How many handshakes occurred?* I live for this stuff. And when Mr. Fernlund saw how good I was, he formally asked me to join the team.

Near the end of the lunch hour I even told a joke. "What do you get if you divide the circumference of a jack-o'-lantern by its diameter? Pumpkin pi." And guess what—they all laughed! Then I had science, and because there is now an odd number of kids in the class, thanks to my arrival, the teacher paired me with Phoebe and Violet indefinitely. Violet didn't look too happy, but Phoebe reminded her that I was excellent at science and therefore my involvement might boost their marks. That seemed to perk Violet up a bit.

For two whole hours I actually forgot all about phys ed and Jared.

BUT BEFORE I KNEW it, last period was upon me. My feet felt like blocks of lead as I headed into the change room. I didn't see Jared, and for a moment I was filled with relief; maybe he was sick, or maybe he'd transferred to another school, or, better still, maybe he was in the hospital in a body cast and wouldn't get out for months. I changed in a bathroom stall, and nobody tried to stop me.

But just as I was pulling up my shorts, I heard him. He has a loud, confident voice, and it boomed through the change room. "Hey, Chong, you coming to basketball tryouts after school?"

"You bet."

I waited in the stall for a long time, my feet up on the toilet seat, until I was sure the other guys had gone to the gym. Only then did I unlock the door and head out to join them.

We played soccer outside and Mr. Stellar put me in goal. Miracle of miracles, I only let one ball in, and our team won. Jared was on the other team. He never even glanced in my direction. This got my hopes up; maybe he'd forgotten all about me.

Wishful thinking.

As the rest of the boys stripped down, I stalled for time, pretending I had a really bad knot in my sneaker. When I glanced up, the change area was almost empty. I could hear the showers running and the boys shouting and laughing.

I grabbed my clothes and headed toward the bathroom stalls, which were on the opposite side of the wall, away from the showers.

Jared leaned against the bathroom sinks, still in his gym uniform, like he was waiting for me. His friend was with him.

"Where do you think you're going?"

"Just needed to pee."

"Bullcrap," he said. Except he didn't say *crap*. "You were trying to avoid the showers again."

"Truth be told, I don't perspire as much as some of you yet, because I am a year younger. Plus, I was a preemie, so physiologically, my glands aren't yet working overtime like yours are—"

"Hey, Paulo, help me out."

Paulo grabbed my arms and held them behind my back.

The clothes I'd been carrying fell to the ground. Jared yanked my shorts down, revealing my underwear. I'd skipped the cat boxers today, opting for basic blue ones instead.

I was terrified. Nothing in my thirteen years had prepared me for a situation like this. Yes, I'd been teased in second grade, but that was peanuts compared to this. And speaking of peanuts, I was pretty sure that what little I had down there had probably shriveled to the size of one.

Jared yanked down my underwear, too.

There was a pause. Then he said, "What the heck is that?" Except he didn't say *heck*.

"It's a wrestling uniform."

To my relief, Jared stopped what he was doing to stare at the outfit Alistair had found for me at the thrift shop. It looked kind of like an old-fashioned one-piece men's bathing suit. It scooped all the way down to just below my belly button, leaving my pasty-white chest and stomach exposed beneath my T-shirt. But the shoulder straps held it securely in place, so it couldn't simply be yanked down. Personally, I felt Alistair's mind had been in top form when he'd suggested it, and it had only cost me two dollars.

"Do you wrestle?" Jared asked.

"No."

"So where'd you get it?"

"A thrift shop."

"Hope you washed it first. What if the previous owner had crotch lice?"

I confess I had not thought of that. It was probably just a coincidence that I suddenly felt an itch down below.

"You are one strange little elf," he stated.

Then he yanked my T-shirt up over my head. I couldn't see a thing. I felt his hand grab one of the straps of my wrestling uniform and pull it down. He grabbed the other strap. I tried my hardest to wriggle out of his grasp, but he was much, much stronger than me, and also I couldn't see, which was very disorienting. I would say it was one of the worst moments of my life, but that wouldn't be true, because after you've watched your mom slowly dying over the course of a year, you have had a lot of "worst moments."

Still, I was in full-on panic mode. I knew I was way beyond any UN-style negotiations or stall tactics. Then—just before he pulled down the other strap—I had a brainwave.

Jared had said he thought Ashley was hot.

And even though I knew she'd hate me forever, I figured it was better than having the entire gym class see my teeny weenie, not to mention the hilarity that would ensue when *that* rumor spread throughout the school. So I played the only card I had left.

"I'm Ashley Anderson's brother!"

Jared let go of my strap. I still couldn't see anything.

"Let him go," he said. Paulo released my arms. I pulled my T-shirt back down. Jared was studying me.

"I didn't know Ashley had a brother."

"I'm not her biological brother. Technically speaking, she doesn't even want me to say *stepbrother*, but I guess that's more or less what I am."

"I'd heard rumors that some weirdo had moved in with her."

"Yes, well. That would be me." He just kept staring at me, like he was thinking something through. It made me uncomfortable. "Um. Can I get changed now?"

"What? Oh, yeah, of course. I was just messing with you. You know, a little initiation ritual."

"Oh. Is that what it was." I bent down to pick up my clothes. I was about to head into a stall when he spoke again.

"What's your name?"

"Stewart."

"You like basketball?"

"On a theoretical level, yes. On a practical level, i.e., actually playing, no. My hand-eye coordination is well below average."

"I have something in mind for you. Meet me tomorrow after school. Outside the gym."

"Why?"

"You'll see." Then he turned and walked out of the bathroom. I ducked into one of the stalls and locked myself in. I let out a huge sigh of relief.

Suddenly his feet reappeared. They stopped right outside my stall. "One last thing," he said through the door.

"What?"

"Tell your sister Jared says hi."

"Oh. Okay."

Then he really, truly walked away.

My bowels loosened and I did what I never do in a public toilet.

I pooped.

ASHLEY

I WAS IN A super-crabby mood after school. First of all, Lauren showed up that morning wearing my skirt. Seriously, she was wearing the *exact skirt* I'd shown her on Saturday when we were in H&M.

"When did you get that?" I asked her at our lockers. Amira, Yoko, and Lindsay were there, too.

"What?" she asked, trying to sound innocent.

"You know what. The skirt."

"Oh. My mom took me shopping yesterday."

"So you bought it even though you knew it was the skirt I wanted."

"Was this the one you wanted? I thought it was the brown one."

I just crossed my arms over my chest and glared at her.

"Well, I was going to get the pants I'd tried on, but you told me they made my butt look big, remember? So then I tried on the skirt, and my mom said it looked great on me."

"And you believed her? She's your *mom*."

Lauren pursed her lips. "I like it. *I* think it looks good on me."

"So do I," Amira said.

"You could still get the brown one," Yoko said to me. She doesn't like it when we fight.

"And have people think I copied her? No, thanks."

Claudia walked past. "Hey, Lauren. Nice skirt."

"Thanks." Lauren threw me a defiant look. I wanted to throttle her.

Then, in English class, Mrs. Donnelly gave us back our essays on *To Kill a Mockingbird*. She'd asked us to write about something of "thematic importance" in the book, and, if I am one hundred percent totally honest, I never got past page fifty. So I'd cut and pasted parts of my essay from Wikipedia, and Mrs. Donnelly figured that out. I got an F. She took me aside after class and told me I had to redo the assignment or risk failing the class.

When I got home, I decided to pamper myself. I made some Red Velvet Cake tea from David's Tea, and I curled up on the couch to watch *Maury*. Shoo-Fly poked his head around the corner and meowed, but he didn't come over even after I called him. Stupid cat.

It was a good episode. It was about a guy who found out, right there on the show, that DNA testing had proved he wasn't the father of his girlfriend's baby, and that the real father was the guy's own brother. I was starting to feel a bit better when *he* entered the room.

"Hello," he said.

I turned up the volume on the TV.

"Why are they all screaming at each other?" he asked.

I turned up the volume a little more.

He picked up Shoo-Fly. "I'm supposed to pass on a message," he yelled. "From Jared."

Even though the brothers were now throwing chairs at each other, I muted the TV.

STEWART

THERE ARE MANY SCIENTIFIC mysteries that are still waiting to be solved. For example, is light a wave or a particle? What causes gravity? Does alien life exist? How did the universe begin? And why is Ashley's behavior so baffling?

One moment she acted like I was invisible; the next she was inviting me to sit down and have a cup of tea. She even got the mug herself, and put in lots of milk and sugar when I asked, because Red Velvet Cake tea is still tea.

"Sit," she said, patting the cushion on the other end of the couch. So I sat. Schrödinger curled up in my lap. I try not to anthropomorphize animals, but I swear he eyed Ashley with suspicion.

"How do you know Jared?" she asked.

"We're in phys ed together."

"And how did you get to talking about me?"

"Well," I began. I tried to figure out how much I should tell her. My mom always said that honesty is the best policy, but then again, she also told her share of white lies. Things like telling our neighbor Mrs. Janowski that, no, she didn't notice she'd gained any weight, when, in fact, Mrs. Janowski had ballooned two dress sizes in six months. Or when she scratched the side of the car when we went shopping and told Dad, "Someone scratched the car in the parking lot." It wasn't a lie, exactly; she just didn't tell him that the "some-one" was her.

"It's kind of a funny story," I began. "See, I thought Jared was about to do something really mean to me, so—and I know you're not going to like this part—I told him you were my sister because last week I'd heard him say you were hot—"

Ashley put her hand up for me to stop. I waited for her to launch into a tirade, something like *I'm not your sister, you freakazoid.* But, scientific mystery that she is, she surprised me. "Jared said I was hot?"

"Yes. So I thought he'd stop picking on me if I—"

"How, exactly, did he say it?"

The question stumped me. "I don't know. He said, 'Ashley Anderson is hot.'"

"But did he say it as kind of a throwaway comment, or did he say it kind of dreamily?"

I had no idea what she was talking about, so I picked one. "Dreamily?"

That seemed to be the right answer, because she grinned from ear to ear. "Did he say anything else about me?"

"Not that I remember. It was a week ago."

"So why are you only telling me now?"

I felt so confused. "I don't know. I didn't know it was significant—"

"Okay, fine," she interrupted. "Tell me about today."

"Well, when he found out we lived together, he became really nice. And then he said, 'Tell your sister Jared said hi.'"

Again, I waited for her to freak out at the word *sister*. But she didn't. She just beamed. It dawned on me that this was the first time I'd seen her genuinely happy since we moved in.

"I guess I should leave you to your show," I said, taking one last sip of my tea.

"You can stay and watch it with me if you want," she replied.

Like I said: scientific mystery.

But I peeled off my socks and stayed.

ASHLEY

AFTER DINNER I WENT to my room to read *To Kill a Mockingbird*. Only I couldn't concentrate. So I went online instead, this time checking out all the photos Jared had posted on Instagram. I think he has a lot of money because he always seems to be posed beside a pool or in a sailboat or in front of the pyramids.

Then I tried again to read—I really did. But my mind kept drifting. I imagined we were boyfriend and girlfriend. We would be one of *those* couples, the kind that would make other people stop and stare because we'd look so fabulous together.

But then I suddenly realized I'd missed an important step. I hadn't passed on a message to Jared in return. So

I hurried out of my room, knocked on Stewart's door, and opened it.

"Stewart—"

I froze. Stewart was sitting on his bed, a hideous brown-and-orange knitted blanket draped over him like a tent.

"Haven't you heard of knocking?" he cried.

"What are you doing?"

"It's personal!"

Oh, *gross!!!* I backed out of his room, yanking the door shut behind me. "Just—tell Jared I said hi back!" I shouted.

Under my breath I added, "Pervert!"

STEWART

I CAME DOWNSTAIRS IN the morning with a bounce in my step because overall, it felt like things were looking up. Even my dad could tell the difference because I hummed a tune over breakfast, and that tune was "My Favorite Things," a song from Mom's second-favorite musical, *The Sound of Music* (her first was *West Side Story*).

"Someone's in a good mood." My dad smiled as he handed me a bowl of porridge (real, not instant). I'd told him over dinner the night before that I'd joined Mathletes, and he was very pleased for me, and so was Caroline, and even Ashley said it seemed like a club that would be happy to have me as a member.

So Dad and I started to sing "My Favorite Things" really

loud, and we both thought it was funny that just as we started singing *"When the dog bites,"* Ashley walked in.

"Want some porridge?" Dad asked her.

"No, thanks," she mumbled. She grabbed a banana from the fruit bowl and left without making eye contact with either of us.

"Oh well," said my dad. "At least she said *thanks*. That's progress."

I thought about telling him what had happened the night before, when Ashley had opened my bedroom door unannounced. I know what she thought I was doing. I wasn't. But even Dad doesn't know about my nightly ritual, and I wasn't sure I wanted to tell him. Then Caroline came into the kitchen and pretty soon we were all singing "My Favorite Things," and I forgot all about it.

WHEN PHOEBE ASKED ME to join her and Violet for lunch, the day got better still. The cafeteria felt a lot less threatening when I had other people to sit with. I laid out my lunch (two egg salad sandwiches, one apple, one banana, one juice box, two Babybels, and six Oreos) on the table.

"Wow. Someone has a big appetite," said Violet. Both she and Phoebe were eating fries and gravy.

"My entire lunch probably doesn't have many more calories than those plates of deep-fried grease you guys are eating," I replied.

"True." Phoebe smiled. "But ours tastes better." She was wearing the best T-shirt ever. It was purple and said,

ALWAYS BE YOURSELF. UNLESS YOU CAN BE A UNICORN. THEN
ALWAYS BE A UNICORN.

I bit into my first egg salad. "Hey, do you guys know a guy named Jared?"

"Jared Mitchell. The new guy. Yeah. Why?" asked Phoebe.

"I think we're becoming friends. He wants me to meet him after school, by the gym."

"Why?"

"I don't know. He was rather cryptic."

"Isn't it basketball tryouts?" asked Violet.

"No offense," said Phoebe, "but you don't seem to have the height for basketball."

"I'm a mathlete, not an athlete," I joked.

But Phoebe didn't laugh. "Just be careful, okay? I don't trust that guy."

"Ditto," said Violet.

"Why not?"

"Just rumors we've heard."

My stomach burbled and churned all afternoon as I thought about what they'd said. If they didn't trust Jared, why should I? Especially after what he'd almost done to me?

I thought about heading home right after school, but I knew there was no point; it wasn't like I could hide from Jared forever. So I made my way to the gym, letting loose a few toots as I went. My mind was whirring. What if this was another initiation ritual? I'd read about enough of them in books or seen them in movies. *What if he wants to beat me on my bare butt with a paddle? What if he wants to dunk my head in a toilet and flush?*

Suddenly a hand clamped down on my shoulder, scaring me so badly I tooted again. "Stewie! There you are!" Jared said. He was in a basketball uniform.

"Actually, I prefer Stewart—"

He gripped my arm. "C'mon." He was really strong. There was nothing I could do but let myself be propelled along as he pulled me into the gym. "Hey, Mr. Stellar! Coach! I found someone. He's perfect, don't you think?"

ASHLEY

I'D HAD A SURPRISINGLY good day. Normally my home ec teacher, Mrs. Golshiri, doesn't like me very much 'cause I talk too much and I burn stuff, but today we got to draw designs for three different outfits. I chose to design casual-but-cute everyday wear. At the end of class, she held up my designs for the whole class to see and said, "These are quite wonderful, Ashley. You clearly have an eye for fashion."

!!!!

It's true I've always had an eye for fashion, but I've only just started doing my own sketches, so I was very flattered. Mrs. Golshiri has talked about the years she spent living in Paris after her family fled the revolution in Iran. Her time in one of the fashion capitals of the world rubbed off on her stylistically speaking, because I can tell that her outfits are of excellent quality, even if they don't hang on her that well, because she is twenty pounds above her ideal weight.

So I was feeling pretty good when I got home. The house was quiet; the nerd-bot wasn't back yet. I grabbed myself an apple and plunked myself on the couch to watch one of my soaps.

I was only about five minutes in when I heard a growl behind me. I remember thinking, *Shopping Cart can't growl like that . . . can he?* just before an enormous, furry brown paw gripped my head.

STEWART

SHE SCREAMED SO LOUD I thought I'd burst an eardrum. Then she leapt off the couch and started pummeling me. She is slender but strong, and taller than me, and also I had zero peripheral vision, so pretty soon I was flat on my back on the carpet. She started kicking me. I tried to shout, but my voice was muffled, and her screams drowned me out.

Then I could hear man-shouts and pounding on the patio doors, and from the eyeholes I caught a glimpse of Ashley running toward the kitchen, screaming, "Daddy, Daddy!" I tried to stand up, but, next thing I knew, Ashley *and* Phil were standing over me, and Phil was wielding a baseball bat. Then another guy appeared behind him, wielding an umbrella.

"Don't hit me!" I shouted. It was hot and smelly inside the head.

"Stewart?" said Phil, peering down at me. I could tell he and the other guy had just come back from a ride, because they were wearing spandex bike shorts and club jerseys.

"Yes!"

Phil lowered the baseball bat. I raised my furry paws and yanked on the head. It came off with a few good tugs.

"Oh. My. GOD! You little freak!" Ashley screamed.

"Stewart, what on earth are you doing?" asked Phil. "Why are you in a bear costume?"

"It's not a bear. It's a bulldog. I'm the new school mascot. Borden Bulldogs."

"You scared the crap out of me!" Ashley wailed. She clung to her dad.

I stood up. "I'm sorry. I didn't mean to scare you. Wait, that's not true. I *did* mean to scare you, but not that bad."

Phil shook his head. "You should never sneak up on anyone like that, Stewart. Especially not a woman."

"I'm sorry," I said, and I really, truly was.

"This is what I have to live with!" Ashley cried, and she buried her face in her dad's shirt.

Phil held her close, stroking her hair. "It's okay, my baby girl, it's okay."

It was a very touching moment, father and daughter reunited, and I felt a bit proud of myself, since, technically speaking, I was the one who'd brought them together.

But it was over in a flash because suddenly Ashley registered the man standing behind her dad.

She pulled away from Phil. "Who's he?"

I recognized the guy; he was the driver of the silver MINI. He looked like he was a few years younger than

Phil, shorter than him by a few inches, with curly brown hair and dark skin and broad shoulders. I wondered if he'd forgotten his own name because he looked to Phil for help.

"This is Michael," said Phil. "He's my . . . new friend."

"Hi, Ashley," Michael said, extending his hand, "I've heard a lot about you."

Ashley's face crumpled. She walked out of the room. Michael stood there with his hand out. I felt awful for the guy, so I extended my own furry paw instead. "Nice to meet you, Michael. I'm Stewart."

Michael mustered a smile. "So I gathered." He shook my furry paw. Then he turned to Phil. "I think I'll head back to your place."

"I'll be there in a minute," Phil said as Michael headed out the patio doors.

"I'm sorry I caused any trouble," I said.

"It's okay, Stewart. I know you didn't mean it." He looked really sad all of a sudden.

"Is Michael the guy you said you were interested in?"

Phil nodded.

"So you got up the guts to ask him out."

"I did. I decided you were right. I *do* have it better than Alan Turing. So I seized the day."

"Good for you."

"We've seen each other a few times now. Turns out we have a lot in common. We both love the outdoors, skiing, kayaking—and biking."

"I like someone, too. Her name's Phoebe. We have a lot in common, too. We're in Mathletes together."

"Well, I wish you luck with her." He glanced toward the ceiling and got that hangdog look on his face again.

"And I wish you luck with *her*," I replied.

"Thanks. See you later, Stewart." He gave my furry shoulder a light punch, then slipped out the patio doors.

ASHLEY

WHEN I TURNED ELEVEN, my dad gave me the best birthday present ever. It was a cream-colored cashmere sweater, and it looked spectacular on me. Everyone said so. I still had my kid-body, and life, like my wardrobe, was simpler. But I loved nice clothes back then, too, and, honestly, it was like that sweater was made for me.

Aside from the sweater, he also gave me an album full of family pictures, which frankly seemed a bit quaint and rustic, since all our photos could be accessed on the computer in a nanosecond. If I'm totally one hundred percent honest, I barely glanced at it.

But lately I've been pulling out that album and studying it, like I'm a detective trying to solve a crime. I look for clues to try to figure out when it all went wrong. The thing is, I never find anything. It's a heartbreakingly *happy* photo album. It's called TO OUR BELOVED DAUGHTER, and it opens with a picture of my mom and dad when they were young and wrinkle-free and my mom has an enormous belly, which, of course, contains me. They are seriously good-looking and well-put-together, as long as you ignore my mom's neon-orange Crocs. They were apparently all she could wear 'cause her feet got all swollen in the last two months of her pregnancy. (Personally, I don't think that is a valid excuse. There is never a valid excuse for ugly shoes.)

In the next photo, Mom and Dad are lying together in a hospital bed, and I am in my dad's arms, wrapped in a blanket. My mom looks exhausted, and I suspect this is pretty accurate, since she was in labor for thirty-one hours. She looks puffy and gross. If I were her, I would have deleted that photo immediately. I don't look much better; my shriveled little face looks more gremlin than human.

But I regress. The point is, in that first photo—and even in the second photo, where my mom and I both look hideous—it is painfully obvious that my parents are head over heels in love. They beam at each other like they can't believe their good luck.

And in all the photos that follow—the three of us on my first Halloween, me wearing a pumpkin costume; my first day of kindergarten; my first dance recital; the three of us on the beach in Maui; the three of us in ski gear up at Whistler; the three of us standing in front of the world's biggest kielbasa outside some town in Alberta when we drove to the Rockies—they still look really happy.

We *all* look really happy.

Now, when I look at the album, I sometimes feel like I'm looking at . . . I don't know, the life of a Russian spy or something. And my dad is the spy, and the people he works for have given him this whole fake identity, and my mom and I are just unsuspecting dupes who've become part of his cover.

But then other times I look at it and I think, *No. What I'm looking at is real.* 'Cause there's no way he could fake it for that many years . . . could he?

My dad has reached out to me a lot. And once or twice, I've tried to reach back. But . . . I don't know. I just can't get past the lie.

I agonize a lot over whether or not I'm a gayist. I mean, on the one hand, we have an LGBT club at our school and I am totally cool with that, even if I've been known to call the president a Tragic behind his/her back because I can't tell if he/she is a boy or a girl thanks to all the shapeless clothing he/she wears and his/her unhelpful name (Sam).

But on the other hand, when it hits close to home, it is a whole different story. I just can't get over the fact that my dad would rather be with men than with Mom.

Meeting Michael just now made that whole part of it very real. I knew he was the guy who'd dropped my dad off this past weekend. The guy who'd leaned in for a kiss.

I felt so depressed all of a sudden. All the good feelings from the day just vanished—*poof!*—like that.

And then, to make things even worse, Spewart knocked on my door. I shoved the photo album under my covers.

"Go away."

"Ashley, I said I'm sorry. Don't you want to know how I became school mascot?"

"No, I do not. I truly do not care."

"Oh. Okay. 'Cause actually it was Jared—"

STEWART

SHE HAD THE DOOR open before I'd finished saying his name. "Jared asked you to be school mascot?"

I nodded. "He told the coach he thought I'd be perfect for the job. The guy who did it last year had a growth spurt. And it's a pretty small costume, so they needed someone who hasn't reached his full height potential yet. The only thing is, the head kind of reeks, like maybe the guy last year had halitosis—"

"Did you give Jared my message?"

"Yes. I did."

"And did he say anything back?"

"Yes. He did."

"What?"

"He said, 'Tell Ashley to go on Facebook tonight so we can chat.'"

Her face went all weird and rubbery, like she was working really hard not to smile. "Did he name a time?"

"He said around eight o'clock."

"That was it?"

"That was it."

"Then why are you still standing here?" She started to close her door, but I put my hand out.

"Can I ask you something?"

"No."

"Why does it bother you so much?"

"What?"

"Your dad being gay."

"Why are you so interested? Maybe 'cause *you're* gay?"

"No, I'm pretty sure I'm straight. All my fantasies are about females—"

She slapped her hands over her ears. "Oh my God! You are so disgusting! You think I don't know what you were doing yesterday under that blanket?"

"Not what you think I was doing."

"Oh, please—"

"I wasn't—"

"You were!"

"I wasn't! I was breathing in my mom's molecules!" I blurted.

She stared at me. "You were what?"

I tried to explain. "The human body is made up of trillions of molecules, right?"

"Maybe. Whatever."

"Molecules are made of atoms. When someone dies, their molecules break down into smaller molecules as well as individual atoms. So, say a carbon atom is part of a molecule in a person's leg. When that person dies, that atom could become part of a molecule in something else, like a blooming flower, or even another human being. Or an oxygen atom in your sandwich could end up in a molecule as part of your brain."

"Ew."

"Right now, as I'm talking to you, you're probably picking up a few Stewart molecules and vice versa."

She slapped her hand over her mouth. "Gross!"

"I don't think it's gross. I think it's kind of beautiful. Everything, and everyone, is interconnected."

Schrödinger wandered up to me and started rubbing against my legs. I picked him up and held him close to me. "Right now I'm breathing in cat molecules."

"You are so weird."

"I don't think it's weird to want to stay connected to my mom in any way I can. A lot of her molecules were floating around our old house, so I always felt connected to her there. But then we moved here, and I had to use a specific object to breathe in her molecules."

"That hideous blanket?"

"It's not hideous. She knitted it. It's called an afghan. When she was sick, she used to lie on the couch with it on top of her. So now I go under it once a day and breathe her in for a while. And I just remember her. It's kind of like I'm collecting a bit of her soul."

Ashley just stared at me. "Still weird. And kind of creepy."

I shrugged. I hadn't expected her to understand. I started to walk to my bedroom, holding Schrödinger.

"But I can't imagine what it must be like to have your mom go and die on you," she continued. "So, I don't know. . . . Maybe, if I was in your shoes, I'd do some weird stuff, too." Then she added, "Not *as* weird, though."

"So why don't you try a little harder with your dad? I know he hurt you, but he's *alive*. He loves you—"

She closed her bedroom door.

Still, it was easily the best conversation Ashley and I had ever had.

ASHLEY

SOMETIMES I WISH MY life was a movie. Not my whole life, but certain moments. Like this morning. When I walked through the front doors of the school, it would have been perfect if it had been filmed in slow motion, with a wind machine blowing my long brown hair back, and a great pop song playing in the background. 'Cause it was that kind of day. The kind of day when I felt like a superstar.

As I strode down the corridor to my locker, I felt full of confidence and *joie de beaver* (that's French for just basically loving life). I was wearing my favorite ensemble: a pair of indigo skinny jeans paired with a loose white top that falls off one shoulder, and a big black belt to cinch it around my tiny waist. Silver ballet flats and a pair of silver hoop earrings brought the whole look together. I am simply stating a fact when I say I looked fantastic.

I'd timed my arrival perfectly, too, because when I got to my locker, Lauren and Claudia were already at theirs. "Oh, hey," I said in a voice that was super-casual yet tinged with an air of mystery. I waited for them to pick up on it.

That was when my movie went a little off-script. Because instead of picking up on my air of mystery, Claudia said, "We were just talking about Ms. Perrault and Mr. Hollinger." She was referring to our French teacher and our history teacher. "Soon-Yi swears she saw them at the Cactus Club in Burnaby last weekend, holding hands across the table."

"Ew," Lauren replied. "Isn't Mr. Hollinger married?"

"Terrible," I said, but vaguely, as if my mind was elsewhere. Then I laughed quietly to myself and shook my head slightly, like I was remembering something funny.

"What?" said Lauren.

"What, what?" I asked, like I had no idea what she was talking about.

"What's so funny?"

"Oh, I was just thinking about the cutest thing Jared said when we were chatting on Facebook last night."

And just like that, we were back on-script. Claudia's eyes widened, and so did Lauren's. I felt a rush of pleasure.

"You were chatting to Jared on Facebook last night?" Lauren asked.

"Mmm-hmm," I said, as if it was no big deal.

"That's kind of weird. I was chatting with him, too."

Again: off-script. Claudia snorted. "Maybe he was

chatting with both of you at the same time," she said, a little too gleefully, if you ask me.

I tried very hard to keep a neutral expression. "What did you chat about?"

"Oh, just homework and stuff."

"Who started the chat?"

Lauren turned beet red, right up to the tips of her ears. "Why is that important?"

Oh, Lauren. Her nonanswer was my answer; *she* had obviously started chatting with *him* when she'd seen he was online. Meanwhile, Claudia's eyes darted from Lauren, back to me. She was clearly enjoying herself.

"He seems like a really nice guy, doesn't he?" I asked Lauren.

"He does."

"Although kind of flirty."

"In what way?"

"Well, you know, saying stuff like, 'How can you not have a boyfriend?' and 'You could be a supermodel.'"

Lauren grew super-quiet. Claudia blew a huge bubble with her gum.

"He didn't say stuff like that to you?" I asked.

"No. We just talked homework."

"Oh . . . sorry."

"It's fine," she said, forcing a smile. "I mean, I didn't ever think he liked me *that* way."

"Okay, 'cause, you know, I wouldn't want to step on your toes or anything."

"You're not."

"Good. 'Cause he asked if we could hang out at my house

after school today. We're meeting at the front doors at three-fifteen."

Lauren pasted on a bright smile. "That's so great, Ashley! I am super-happy for you!"

"Thanks, Lauren," I said, meaning it. Then I let myself get truly excited for a moment. "Oh my God, Jared Mitchell is coming to my house!"

I grabbed Lauren's arms and she grabbed mine, and we jumped up and down, squealing in unison. And even though I knew it wasn't totally genuine on her part, I appreciated the effort.

Claudia, on the other hand, just sucked her bubble back in and snorted again.

I made a mental note to freeze her out for a few days.

WHEN I ARRIVED AT the front doors after school, Jared was already there, waiting for me. He looked adorable in jeans, Vans, and a white button-up shirt with a baby-blue V-neck sweater on top.

Sometimes my eye for fashion is a curse, because being at Borden Secondary is a daily assault on my eyes. Monday to Friday I walk through a sea of fashion don'ts. The boys are the worst offenders—most of them just don't seem to care that they look like total slobs.

But not Jared. His wavy dark hair has that "just got out of bed" look that I happen to know takes a very long time and lots of hair product to perfect. Ditto the way his white button-up shirt is untucked on one side; this is a well-executed move by someone who has looked at his share of fashion magazines. He clearly puts effort into his effortless look, and that says a lot about a person's character.

"Hey," he said when he saw me. Then he grinned. *Oh, that smile!*

"Hi."

"I like your outfit."

"Thanks. I like yours, too."

"So, which way do we go?"

I nodded north, and we started to walk together. The area around the school was full of kids heading home, and again I had that movie-star feeling, knowing that many eyes were upon us. I could even see Claudia and Lauren and Yoko and Amira by one of the side entrances, and I knew they were watching us. I also knew that Jared and I looked very, very good together. Jared is almost six feet tall, and I am five-six, which is, according to my magazines, a perfect height difference.

I tried to think of something to say, but suddenly I felt super-shy. I kind of hoped he'd ask me questions about my-self, but he didn't, so finally I said, "What school did you go to before Borden?" Even though I already knew.

"Saint Patrick's."

"Private school?"

He just nodded.

"And why did you transfer?"

"It wasn't by choice. I was kicked out."

I knew this, too. The rumor around school was that he'd hit someone. "How come?"

He shrugged. "Let's just say I dealt with someone who needed dealing with. Guy was a colossal turd, and everyone

126

knew it. But I'm the one who paid the price." His beautiful chocolate-brown eyes clouded over, which made him even more irresistible; broodiness was a very good look on him.

"That's not fair," I said as we turned onto my block.

"Totally. And now I'm stuck at a crap school."

Even though I dissed Borden all the time, I felt kind of insulted. "It's not *all* crap."

"No." He grinned. "You go there."

!!!!!

We arrived at my house. I unlocked the front door and we headed inside. All I could think about was that I had the next couple of hours alone with the best-looking boy at school, which made me both excited and butterfly-tummied all at once.

That's when I heard "Hey, Ashley. Hey, Jared!"

I'd forgotten all about Spewart.

STEWART

I HUNG OUT WITH Ashley and Jared in the family room. They sat next to each other on the couch, and I sat in my mom's chair. I think they were feeling really shy because they hardly said a word.

"First game's coming up at the end of next week," I said to Jared, trying to keep the conversation going. "I've been working on my routine. Want to see?"

Jared shrugged, still feeling shy, I guess. So I peeled off my socks and busted some moves for them, including (if I do say so myself) an excellent rendition of "The Worm."

When I was done, Ashley had her face hidden in her hands. But Jared was smiling. "You're gonna knock 'em dead, Stewie."

"It's Stewart," I said, but I was pleased.

"Don't you have homework to do?" Ashley said.

"No, I finished it at lunch."

Ashley turned to Jared. "We could go to your house."

"No, we can't. My folks pay our housekeeper extra to watch me like a hawk."

Ashley and I had very different responses to this. Mine was "Why do you need to be watched like a hawk?"

Hers was "Wow. You have a full-time housekeeper?"

Jared just stood up and wandered over to the mantel. "What's with all the figurines?"

"They're Stewart's," Ashley said, like she was trying to distance herself from an unpleasant situation.

"They were my mom's," I told him. "She collected them. Each one has a story behind it. For example, this one"—I picked up a delicate fairy perched on a toadstool—"belonged to my mom's great-grandmother. And this one," I continued, picking up a boy with a fishing rod, "is a real Royal Doulton that my grandma, my mom's mom, gave her on her wedding day. And *this* one," I said, picking up Dopey, one of Snow White's seven dwarves, "is Dopey. I bought it for my mom a couple of years ago."

Jared sneezed. *"Achoo!"*

"Bless you."

"Achoo!"

"Bless you."

"Achoo!"

"Bless you."

"Do you guys have a cat?"

"He does," Ashley said.

"I'm allergic."

I got down on my hands and knees and looked under the couch. "Yup. There's the culprit. Come on out, Schrödinger."

"Put him in your room," Ashley snapped. "And while you're at it, put yourself in your room, too."

"It's okay," Jared said. "I should get going anyway. My folks will be home soon." He looked at Ashley. "Walk me to the door?"

"Of course." Then, over her shoulder to me: "You. *Stay where you are.*"

So I did. I pulled Schrödinger onto my lap. He flipped onto his back and stretched out all four paws and purred loudly as I rubbed his belly.

After what felt like a long, long time, Ashley returned. "Oh my *God!*" she said. "Could you not have left us alone for, like, five minutes?"

"What? He's my friend, too."

"No. He's not. He's your acquaintance. Don't be so dense, Stewart. I think he likes me, and I like him. If you wreck it for me, I swear I'll kill you."

Two death threats in under a week!

"And don't you dare tell my mom that Jared came over."

"Why not?"

"She has this stupid rule that I'm not allowed to have boys over unless an adult's home. It's super-harsh and old-fashioned."

I thought about this for a moment. "But if he was visiting *me,* it would be okay."

"Yes," said Ashley, "which is totally unfair—" She stopped as what I was saying dawned on her.

"So if, in the future, *I* invited Jared to come over . . ."

"That wouldn't be breaking any rules. Stewart, you're a genius!"

"Not really. I'm just using some tools I learned when I was a part of the Model UN. Sometimes we had to bend certain rules to get what we wanted. For example, when I represented Denmark, we had to make a few small financial promises to Greece before they'd get on board with our humanitarian efforts in Bangladesh—"

"Okay, stop talking now." She flopped onto the couch and turned on the TV.

"Of course," I continued, "you have to promise me something in return."

"You're bribing me?"

"I prefer to call it *negotiating*."

"What? What do you want?"

"You have to agree to everything I say at dinner tonight."

"*Pfft*. Fine. Whatever. Now, go."

So I went, carrying Schrödinger in my arms. But I was smiling.

Because I was already hatching a plan.

SOME PEOPLE WOULD SAY that Ashley's nonexistent relationship with her dad is none of my business. Some people would say it's something only they can work out.

My mom would never, ever have said that.

Before she had me, Mom was a family counselor. Ms. Janice Beaudry, her maiden name. It took her a long time to go back to work after I was born (I suspect because I took a lot of her time and energy), but when I was eight, she went back part-time. She saw a lot of families from all walks of life, parents and kids who were having problems getting along for a billion different reasons. Mom loved her work, and she was good at it. She had a sign in her office: I DON'T CARE HOW POOR A MAN IS; IF HE HAS FAMILY, HE'S RICH. I thought she'd made it up, but apparently it was written by a couple of TV writers, for an episode of a show called *M*A*S*H*.

I'm not an expert like she was. But I felt that at the very least I could try to nudge things along with Ashley and Phil, because (1) when you've lost a parent, you don't have much patience for people who complain about theirs, and (2) self-ishly speaking, this wasn't just *her* family anymore; it was mine. And I wanted us all to get along.

Which is why I said the following over our dinner of frit-tata and salad that night: "Ashley and I think it would be nice to invite Phil to dinner."

Ashley started to choke on a piece of frittata. My dad gave her a couple of thumps on the back. She picked up her water glass and drank, glaring at me the whole time. But she didn't say anything.

A meaningful look passed between Caroline and my dad. "Well," Caroline said, "I'm impressed. Surprised, but impressed."

"We had a long talk," I continued as Ashley kept sipping her water, "and I convinced Ashley that we can't shut Phil out of this new family that we're trying to build. He needs to be a part of it, too." I smiled, convinced that Mom would have given me a gold star for that little speech.

Caroline looked quizzically at Ashley; I think she

suspected the idea hadn't come from her. But all she said was "Well. This is incredibly mature of you, sweetheart."

"It really is," added my dad.

Ashley's nostrils flared and I could tell she wanted to rip my head off. But visions of Jared must have been dancing in her head because all she said was, "You don't need to look so shocked. I've always been mature for my age."

"I'll call Phil after dinner and arrange it," said Caroline. "Unless, Ashley, you'd rather—"

"No!" Ashley said. "You can talk to him."

I helped myself to another big piece of frittata and smiled on the inside.

Once I've graduated from university? The UN should hire me for real. I think I could solve a lot of the world's problems quite handily.

ASHLEY

IT'S JUST OVER A week since Jared first walked me home, and the rumor mill at school has officially started. *Everyone* is talking about me and Jared, and the fact that we are possibly, maybe, *ohmygodIhopeso* becoming "an item." I am getting tons of envious glances in the corridors, even from girls in tenth grade, which is a wonderful high.

Even though Jared and I don't have any classes together, we do have the same lunch break, and he's joined me in the cafeteria *every day*! The first time, Lauren was already sitting with me, and she *so* did not grab a clue; she stayed with us the whole time. But when Jared sat down with us again the next day, I said, "Um, Lauren? Don't you have something to discuss with Claudia?"

"No," she said.

"I'm pretty sure you do," I replied, staring at her. "So buh-bye."

She finally got the hint and left.

Jared laughed. "You have her well trained. Does she roll over and play dead, too?"

"Yes, but she isn't fully housebroken," I replied, and we both laughed, and I felt *so good* because normally I only think of good comebacks two or three days later.

Still, I felt kind of guilty when I saw Lauren at her locker later. Her eyes looked red and her skin looked splotchy, like she'd been crying.

"I didn't mean to be so harsh earlier," I said. "I just really wanted some time alone with Jared."

"It's okay. I should have clued in."

"Yeah, you should have. But I love you anyway."

"I love you, too."

We hugged, and all was well again.

I have to try harder to be kind to Lauren. After all, she's not as fortunate as I am. And she's my best friend.

But back to the important stuff: Jared was out of town for the weekend, but he came over twice after school this week. Then, on Friday after school, I went to the gym to watch the Borden Bulldogs' first home game. I'm not big into basketball, but I'm big into Jared. I sat between Lauren and Claudia. The guys were warming up on the court, and I was admiring Jared's muscular calves and shivering, 'cause my jacket was still in my locker and our gym is freezing.

Then the most amazing thing in the world happened.

Jared ran up to me and handed me his warm-up jacket. In front of everyone!! I felt so cozy and happy for the rest of the game I didn't even care that the Bulldogs lost.

Or that Spewart totally humiliated himself in front of the entire school.

STEWART

HAVING NO PERIPHERAL VISION is very disorienting. I know, because on Friday afternoon I experienced it firsthand.

I was also drenched in sweat. Beads of moisture dripped into my eyes, making *any* vision difficult. Only if I looked straight ahead could I see clearly, and what I saw were hundreds of people. All staring at me. All waiting to see what I'd do next.

I was terrified.

BUT ALLOW ME TO backtrack. The rest of the week that led up to my moment of terror had been exceptionally good. In fact, if I were to do a bar chart of my time at Borden so far, it would look like this:

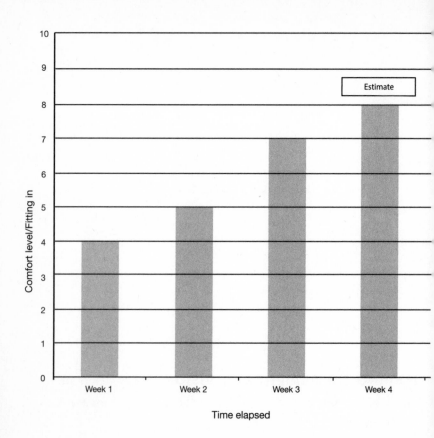

Time elapsed

Week four hasn't happened yet, but I estimated it based on the previous data. Since Jared has taken me under his wing, even phys ed is fine. And Mathletes is just about the best thing that has ever happened to me. I fit in with Phoebe Schmidt, Walter Krasinski, George Hung, Oscar Bautista, Clark Fowler, and Aryama Daliwal. On Wednesday, we had our first actual competition against a high school on the west side called Trafalgar. Even though they had this one kid named Farley who was almost as good at math as I am, we won easily. On the way home on the bus, I sat beside Phoebe, so close I could smell her deodorant. "What did zero say to eight?" I asked her.

"What?"

"Nice belt."

She laughed. I wanted to impress her, so I also told her that I was the new school mascot. "Jared Mitchell got me the job."

But she just said, "Watch out for him."

"Jared? Why?"

"He's got psycho eyes. You know, like he's kind of dead inside. Like he's constantly trying to figure out how a normal person would react. Pretty on the outside but hollow on the inside."

"I think you've watched too many *CSI*s."

"Possibly. But I also have parents who are psychologists, and they've taught me to trust my instincts. That guy gives me a bad feeling. Like, why does he just suddenly show up at our school?"

"*I* just suddenly showed up at your school."

"Yeah, but your story makes sense. *He* showed up 'cause his big, expensive private school kicked him out."

"But we don't know why."

"No. But chances are, they had a good reason."

I didn't share Phoebe's concerns. True, I hadn't met Jared in the best possible way, but he'd been really nice to me lately. He'd come to our house a couple more times after school, and as per my agreement with Ashley, I didn't tell. I even went upstairs once and let them have some privacy in the family room. I left my door open, and I could hear them talking and giggling. When it got really quiet at one point, I stomped noisily back downstairs. I've taken sex ed. I know the cold, hard facts. We don't need a teen pregnancy on our hands.

When the bus pulled up to our stop, Phoebe and I hopped off. "See you tomorrow, Stewart." She headed east. I watched her go. For the first time, I noticed that her head is disproportionately bigger than the rest of her body. I guess it's housing that big, beautiful brain.

So, yes. It had been a really good week leading up to Friday.

Except for one small thing.

On Thursday after school I noticed that one of my mom's figurines was missing. I counted once, twice, three times, but sure enough, Dopey was gone. At first I figured Schrödinger had knocked it off and batted it under a piece of furniture, but I looked under all the chairs and couches and tables, and I couldn't find it anywhere.

Next I suspected Ashley.

"As if I would ever touch those hideous things," she said when I asked her. "They give me the creeps."

I hope it shows up soon. It was my gift to my mom on her last Mother's Day. She'd told me that sometimes the chemo made her feel dopey. Get it? It was supposed to be a joke, a way of bringing a bit of levity to a bad situation.

Some people might have found it tasteless. Not Mom. She thought it was hilarious.

*   *   *

BUT BACK TO FRIDAY. I was still frozen to the spot, peering out at the crowds, when Coach Stellar yelled in my ear. Well, he was yelling in the dog's ear, but I could still hear him. "What are you waiting for? Get out there!" The kids were getting restless, and the halftime clock was ticking down. My stomach gurgled in an alarming way. I wanted to make a dash for the change room.

Then I caught sight of my dad in the stands. My heart swelled, because I knew he had to take half a day off work to come see me. I saw Ashley, too, sitting nowhere near my dad, between her friends Lauren and Claudia.

Then I spotted Phoebe, sitting with Violet, and my heart swelled again.

I took a deep breath. I thought of my mom. I reminded myself that I was doing this for her.

Then I jogged to the center of the gym floor.

With the music blasting through the speakers, I did a pirouette and gave a little bow. The crowd cheered. "Borden Bulldogs! Borden Bulldogs!"

My stomach gurgled a little less. I started skipping up and down the gym floor, clapping my hands together over my head like I'd practiced at home. The crowd started clapping with me. I did "The Swim," followed by "The Dougie." In a moment of improvisation, I grabbed a random ninth-grade girl from the lower bleachers and got her to dance with me.

Then I did what I instantly knew would become my signature move. I got down on the ground and started doing "The Worm." The crowd went nuts. I kept going even after the music ended, squirming around on the gym floor. Finally,

Mr. Stellar had to run out and shout at me that the game was about to resume. "Get the hell off the court, Inkster!"

I skipped to the sidelines just as Jared and four of his teammates trotted out for the third quarter.

And I was so glad I had the costume on, because suddenly I was crying my eyes out under the dog head. I couldn't stop picturing my mom, and how happy this moment would have made her. She was never anything but proud of me, but I also know that she worried about me. I'd heard her conversations with Dad, late at night, through the vent in my room.

"He's safe for now at Little Genius Academy, but what about down the road? He has to function in the real world, too. . . . I know he'll be an amazing adult, but it's those in-between years that scare me. Young people can be so cruel. . . ."

So I was crying because I couldn't help but wish more than anything that she could've seen me, wearing a dog costume and doing "The Worm" across the gym floor.

It would have filled her with relief to see me acting so normal.

ASHLEY

I FELT A LITTLE bit glum when I woke up on Saturday morning. Call it post-amazing-moment-with-Jared letdown, I guess. I didn't see him after the game 'cause the players had to go get yelled at by Mr. Stellar for a long time in the change room. But I still had his jacket, so I brought it home with me. True and slightly embarrassing confession: I snuggled with it in bed. It smelled like a mix of Jared's deodorant and BO. It was heavenly. If I believe Stewart, I guess it means I was breathing in a few of Jared's molecules. Which is super-creepy and super-romantic all at the same time.

Anyway, I drifted back to sleep for a while longer, then got up and did a yoga podcast in my room. I was heading downstairs for breakfast when I heard Mom and Lenny bickering in the kitchen.

"It looks like a typhoon hit in here," Mom said.

"I'll get to it," Leonard replied. "I always do."

"Yes, but sometimes you don't get to it till a full day later. And since I can't stand seeing the sink filled with dirty pots and pans, I usually wind up doing them myself."

I sat down on the stairs to eavesdrop. I'd never heard them argue before. It was unsettling *and* entertaining.

"Oops," said Leonard. "Did someone wake up on the wrong side of the bed?"

"I'm serious, Len. Ditto all the socks you and Stewart leave lying around, even on tabletops. It's disgusting. Is it so hard to pick them up and put them in the hamper?"

My sentiments exactly! I wanted to shout.

There was a pause. Then Leonard said, "I didn't realize it bothered you so much."

"Well, it does."

"I guess we were a little more relaxed in our old house."

There was another silence. I wasn't even in the room with them and I could tell my mom was fuming. "Are you suggesting I'm anal-retentive?" she said. "Just because I like a tidy house?"

"I'm suggesting," Leonard said, "that you are a beautiful, smart, perfect specimen who happens to like things just so."

Wow. Even I had to admit that was pretty smooth. Mom clearly thought so, too, because I heard her giggle. "How dare you make me laugh when I'm still angry with you."

Suddenly my phone dinged. I pulled it from my pocket; it was a text from Jared. *Want 2 C a movie tonight?*

I almost screamed. I texted back. *Sure.*

Great. I'll come by at 8.

I hopped up and ran into the kitchen. "Omigod, omigod! You won't believe what just happened!" Then I froze in my tracks because they were *making out* in front of the coffee-maker. I made a retching sound, and they pulled apart.

"What?" Leonard asked. "What happened?"

"Jared's just invited me to a movie tonight!"

"Jared?" Mom asked. "Who's Jared?"

"Only the hottest guy at our school."

"I hope he's more than just hot," said Leonard, which was a comment only a non-hot person would make.

"Oh, he is. He's also rich!"

Mom raised an eyebrow, and I knew she thought I was being, like, surfacey, so I said, "He's also really nice. Please, can I go? He'll come by at eight."

She and Leonard shared a look. "Eight should be okay," Mom said. "We'll just get your dad over here a bit earlier so we can still have a nice, long visit."

My heart sank.

I had totally forgotten about my dad. Tonight was the night they'd agreed on for him to come to dinner.

"Fine, but he has to be gone by quarter to eight," I said.

"Ashley, I am not going to ask your dad to leave the house at a prescribed time. That's just plain rude."

"Agreed," said Leonard.

Who asked you? I wanted to shout. Instead, I said, "He should be grateful he's coming over at all!"

"*Ashley.*" Mom said my name in that tone that meant "Shut up right now or there will be consequences." And I did

145

not want consequences, since they would almost certainly involve not letting me go to a movie with Jared.

"Fine. But I'm leaving the moment Jared rings the bell."

"I have the feeling none of us will mind," she replied.

"Good!"

It wasn't until I was halfway up the stairs that I realized I'd just been insulted by my very own mother.

I WAS UP IN my bathroom, brushing on a little bit more of my new lilac eye shadow, when the doorbell rang. It was 5:30 p.m. on the dot.

Dad had come to the front door and rung the bell. I couldn't help thinking how weird that was. Ringing the bell to get into the house that you'd lived in for over twelve years, the house you still half owned.

"Ashley, please answer the door," Mom hollered from the kitchen. I pretended I didn't hear her. "Ashley!"

Before you could say "nerd-face," Stewart was poking his head into my room. "C'mon, your dad's here."

"You go," I told him, still checking myself out in the mirror. "I'm not ready yet."

"Ashley Anderson, if you don't get your butt down here right now, you are grounded immediately!" my mom shouted.

Mom belongs to this human-rights organization called Amnesty International. She is always doing letter-writing campaigns and speaking at events for free, and going on about different groups of people who are persecuted in other parts of the world just because of their racial background or sexual orientation, or even just for being female. Which

I found totally one hundred percent ironic, since who was doing the persecuting *right now*?

But I followed Stewart down the stairs. I let him open the door. I stood back a bit, my arms crossed over my chest, which was a little bit bigger than usual 'cause I was wearing the gel bra I'd bought with some of my birthday money.

My dad stood on the doorstep, grinning nervously. He looked good. But then, he always looks good. He wore a pair of designer jeans that fit him really well and a button-up purple shirt under the slate-gray V-neck sweater I'd given him for his birthday two years ago.

"Hi, Stewart. Hi, Ashley."

"Phil, how nice to see you," said Stewart, sounding like an adult in a midget's body. They shook hands. "Please, come in."

Dad took a step toward me. I tried to turn away, but I wasn't quick enough. He put his arms around me, even though he must have seen the scowl on my face. He hugged me tight and kissed the top of my head and murmured, "Ashley, my girl," and out of nowhere my eyes welled up and it took everything in my power not to burst into tears, because he used to hug me *all the time* back when things were normal; we were a very huggy family, and it felt so familiar and comfortable and warm and safe. And just as quickly, my eyes dried up and I felt a wave of fury again because he was the one who'd ruined it all.

I wriggled out of his grasp, which made him look sad, but tough bananas. Stewart, still playing host, said, "Caroline and Leonard are in the kitchen." So Dad went into the kitchen and said hi to them, and he even gave Mom a kiss on the cheek. He dropped off a bottle of wine and his world-famous Caesar salad.

"Why don't the three of you sit in the family room?" Mom suggested. "Dinner will be ready soon." As we left the kitchen, I heard her say under her breath to Leonard, "And he'd better not find any stray socks."

"He won't," Leonard replied. "Stewart and I were on high sock alert."

Stewart sat in his ugly purple-and-green chair. Dad and I sat on opposite ends of the leather couch.

"You look very pretty tonight, Ashley," Dad said.

Not to brag, but he was speaking the truth. I was wearing this adorable little blue-and-gold dress that I'd bought last year and recently revamped with my sewing machine, making it shorter and adding a gold ribbon around the waist. "Thanks."

"She's going on a date tonight," Stewart added. How he even knew this was a mystery to me; he must've been listening in earlier when Lauren was over to help me choose the perfect outfit.

"Shut up, Stewart," I said.

I knew Dad was dying to ask me a bunch of questions, but all he said was "Would I like him?"

Before I could even open my mouth, Stewart said, "You'll get to meet him later. He's picking her up at eight."

"But you'll probably be gone by then," I added.

Dad just grinned. "Don't count on it."

Shoot me now.

Then I had a happier thought. To look at my dad, you

would never guess he's gay. So if Jared did see my dad—and I would make sure it was for no more than a nanosecond—he'd probably just assume he was straight.

"Hey, Stewart, I'd love to see your electric bicycle after supper," Dad said.

"Sure thing. It's really coming along."

Dad looked around the room. "I see you've made some changes in the decor."

"We brought this chair with us," Stewart said. "And the afghan blanket you're leaning against, which was knit by my mom."

"I take it the figurines are yours as well?"

"Indeed they are." Stewart beamed, like he was actually proud of the sheer amount of ugliness he'd brought into our home.

"They're very . . . interesting," said my dad. He caught my eye. And for the second time in one night, a wave of the old love I used to have for him washed over me, because I knew that look. It was a look we'd shared many times before, like when Mom would model a new outfit that she'd dared to buy without having me or Dad along. It was a look that said *Yikes*.

We both felt the moment. Dad started to laugh. Just a little bit at first, but next thing we knew, we were both laughing so hard tears were running down our faces. And I guess Stewart didn't want to be left out, because he started to laugh, too.

And that's how Mom found us when she called us to the table, laughing our heads off, and even though I still think

Stewart is a total stinkpot, I had to admit (but never out loud) that having my dad over for dinner wasn't the worst idea in the world.

The meal flew by. Mom and Leonard put on a feast of barbecued salmon and roasted veggies, and I ate more than I usually do, although I avoided Dad's salad 'cause I didn't want my breath to smell like garlic. The conversation wasn't so bad, either, except they talked a little too much about politics.

Then Stewart had to go there.

"So, Phil. Tell us more about your new boyfriend."

Dead silence.

Dad cleared his throat. "Well. His name is Michael."

"What does he do?"

"He's a costume designer. He's worked on some really big films." He blushed a little. "And he's an awfully nice person."

"I'm happy for you, Phil," my mom said, sounding mostly sincere.

Then the doorbell rang.

Jared. I saw the look that passed between my dad, my mom, and Leonard; they were all dying to lay eyes on him. "Stay where you are," I ordered them. "And do *not* embarrass me."

I walked to the door, smoothing my dress, and opened it. Jared stood under the porch light. He wore jeans, a long-sleeved white shirt, and a black leather jacket. He looked fantastic.

"You ready?"

"I am," I said, and grabbed my impractical-but-cute gray wool coat, ready to take off.

"Ashley, introduce us to your friend before you go, please!" my mom yelled from the dining room.

I rolled my eyes. "Do you mind?"

"Not at all."

So I took him through to the dining room and introduced him. All the grown-ups had totally goofy smiles on their faces.

"Hey, Jared," Stewart said as he pulled up an extra chair. "Take a load off. We were just talking about Phil's—"

"Job," I almost shouted. "He's in advertising."

"Oh. Cool," said Jared, and to my horror, he sat down. "Would I know any of your stuff?"

"Have you seen those cheese ads on TV?" my dad asked.

"You mean the one with the dancing cheddar?"

"One and the same."

"That ad cracks me up."

"Well, it's one of ours."

"Must be interesting work."

"It is, most of the time."

Jared turned to my mom. "Ashley didn't tell me you were *the* Caroline Anderson. My folks watch you on the news all the time."

"Well, that's good to hear," Mom said. "Leonard's the producer, making it all happen behind the scenes."

"What do your parents do?" asked Leonard.

"Dad's a corporate lawyer. Mom's a stockbroker."

"And what are your interests, Jared?" Mom asked. Honestly, at this rate we were never going to get out of here.

"Jared's on the basketball team," Stewart said.

"Oh, yeah? What position?" asked my dad.

"Power forward."

I started to edge out of the room, hoping Jared would follow. "We'd better get going or we'll miss the movie."

Jared stood up. "It was a pleasure to meet you all."

"You too, Jared," Mom said. Then she gave me a thumbs-up when he turned his back. Totally embarrassing.

A minute later, we were outside, walking toward the bus stop. I breathed deeply, 'cause I could finally relax. "Pretty cool that your mom and dad and stepdad can actually have a meal together," he said.

"Yeah, I guess."

"Why'd your parents split up?"

"They just didn't get along anymore," I lied.

"My parents have *never* gotten along. But they stay together anyway." He grinned. Then he took my hand. He didn't let it go the whole way to the bus stop. And he paid my bus fare.

I knew right then and there: I was in love.

STEWART

WE PUT UP OUR Christmas tree today even though it is only November 30. Ashley protested because she said (1) it was way too early, and (2) our tree is plastic and she "won't be associated with such total one hundred percent tackiness." But she and Caroline don't buy their real tree till a week before Christmas, which is nuts. I tried to explain that in our family, we are Christma-holics, and therefore we like getting an early start—we can't get enough of the holiday season! Before it could turn into an argument pitting Dad and me against Caroline and Ashley, Caroline made the suggestion that we have two trees this year: our plastic one, which could go up in the family room immediately, and their real one, which could go up a few weeks later in the living room. I asked Caroline if she had ever been on the Model UN team when she was in school because her diplomacy skills are excellent. She just laughed and said no, but that working in the newsroom required a lot of diplomacy, especially when it came to "a certain arrogant sportscaster."

While Ashley refused to participate in "this total disregard for estheticians" (I think she meant *aesthetics*), Dad and Caroline and I put on Christmas music and assembled the tree and hung all the decorations we had got out of our storage locker on the North Shore the day before. My mom was a serious crafter, so most of our decorations are homemade and involve a lot of glitter, glue, and Popsicle sticks.

The tree looked really good. Caroline brought me a peppermint hot chocolate with marshmallows and said, "You've done your mom proud," and my eyes filled with tears even though I'd promised myself that yesterday would be the last day for tears, at least for a little while. But it's not that easy to turn off the faucet.

See, yesterday was the second anniversary of my mom's death.

I remember the day she died like it was yesterday. I know that sounds like a cliché, but it's true, and I bet anyone else who's experienced the death of a loved one would vouch for me. She'd been in the palliative-care unit at the hospital for two weeks. *Palliative care* is basically the end of the road in medical terms. It means the experts have agreed that there are no last-ditch medical miracles coming your way. Your goose is about to be cooked. Your bucket is about to be kicked. Your farm is about to be bought. It means the doctors and nurses will do their best to make you as comfortable as possible as you drift toward death. During those two weeks, she could still talk to me when I visited, which was every day.

But on the last day, she could no longer talk. She was drifting in and out of consciousness. My dad had gone to talk to the nurses, so I did the only thing I could think of. I crawled into the narrow bed beside her and put my arms around her. She felt so tiny, like a little bird. Her bones were right under her skin. I lay there and breathed in as many of her molecules as I could, so that a part of her could live on in me. I did that for a long time, even after my dad came back into the room.

Mom died later that night.

The first two weeks weren't so bad. There was so much to do, and a ton of people came by with casseroles and cards. Her memorial service was packed; my mom was just one of those women who made an impression on everyone. There were people from her work, both coworkers and patients; people from Dad's newsroom and my school; her crafting friends, her book club gals, her rowing team; and half the people from our neighborhood, because Mom talked to every-one wherever she went. Even some of the staff from our local coffee shop showed up.

But then the people disappeared and went back to their daily lives, and suddenly Mom's absence hung around our house like a bad smell. That first year was not good, for me or for Dad.

This year was better. But there are still tons of days when I feel impossibly sad. Dr. Elizabeth Moscovich has assured me that this is normal, and will continue to be normal.

But the second half of November was the worst. I had

thought that this year might be a bit better since (1) another year has passed, and (2) we've made so many changes. But to be honest, I think the changes made it even worse. By moving away from everything Mom knew, it's like we abandoned her and her memory. If she were here, she would tell me that's ridiculous, because that's the kind of woman she was, but still. I can't stop the feelings from happening.

When the third week of November rolled around, I started to feel uneasy. It was a good November on paper: Mathletes kicked butt, I got to spend a lot of time with Phoebe, and other kids had started talking to me because I have gained a certain cachet as the school mascot. But none of this mattered. With every passing day, I felt more anxious, as if a shadowy but unseen monster was following me. I had to call Dr. Elizabeth Moscovich at least six times on her private number so that she could calm me down.

Finally—yesterday—the anniversary itself arrived. Caroline made us bacon and eggs for breakfast. Dad and I were both really subdued. She sat at the table with us and took my hand.

"Would you like me to come today, too?"

"It's nice of you to offer, Caroline. But I think I'd rather just go with my dad, if you don't mind." I didn't tell her that in a million years I couldn't imagine bringing her along.

"I understand." She didn't let go of my hand, which made it awkward to try to eat. "You know you can always talk about her, Stewart. Your dad and I talk about your mom quite a bit, when we're alone. But we can talk about her anytime. It's important to keep her memory alive."

"Thank you." I finally shook my hand free.

Ashley came into the kitchen a few minutes later and grabbed a banana. She glanced over at the table. "You made him bacon and eggs for breakfast?" she said to Caroline. "You never make me eggs during the week!"

"Stewart's mom died two years ago today."

Ashley opened her mouth. Then she closed it again. Then she opened it. Then she closed it. She turned to leave the room. Then she turned back and grabbed me from behind, like she was about to give me the Heimlich maneuver.

It was only after she'd left that I realized it was her version of a hug.

TWO YEARS AGO, DAD and I sprinkled Mom's ashes in a few of her favorite places, like Whytecliff Park (in the water), the steps of the Vancouver Art Gallery (discreetly), Ambleside Park (also in the water), and Kidsbooks in Edgemont Village (on the sidewalk outside, also discreetly).

So, on the second anniversary of her death, we spent the morning visiting all of her favorite places. Dad even bought me a book that was recommended by one of the staff at Kidsbooks, *The Absolutely True Diary of a Part-Time Indian* by Sherman Alexie.

Then we went to the storage locker. I spent a long time there, going through boxes and picking out a few more things to bring to our new house. On top of the Christmas tree and the decorations, I took a few of Mom's cookbooks and a smaller painting she'd done, this one of a bowl of fruit. I figured no one could be offended by a bowl of fruit, no matter where we chose to hang it.

After that, we were hungry, so we stopped for lunch at Thomas Haas in North Van. I had dessert for lunch and a big hot chocolate to go with it. It was a good way to warm ourselves up before we headed to Mom's bench.

My mom doesn't have a plot in a cemetery. Instead, she has a park bench. The dedication reads, JANICE BEAUDRY-INKSTER: NUMBER ONE MOTHER, NUMBER ONE WIFE; KIND, LOVING, AND FULL OF LIFE. (I helped Dad come up with the rhyme.)

We brought a huge bouquet of her second-favorite flowers, lilies (her favorite were peonies, but they're hard to come by in November). We left them on the bench. Then Dad and I flipped a coin. He got his private time on the bench first, and I wandered out of hearing distance. When it was my turn, he did the same.

During my private time, I filled her in on all the good stuff that's been happening to me. I like to keep these one-sided conversations light and upbeat, on the off chance she can actually hear me. Scientifically speaking, this is highly improbable, but I prefer to keep the door open just in case.

So I didn't tell her that another one of her figurines was missing. This time it was one of her all-time favorites, a Royal Doulton Bunnykins, featuring an adorable bunny on his hind legs, in a painter's smock, in front of an easel. Mom loved it because she loved bunnies and she loved painting. "It combines two of my favorite things," she used to say.

I didn't tell her I'd confronted Ashley, who'd simply said, "I haven't touched your stupid figurines." And I didn't tell her about what I'd overheard last week when I was in the change room after a game. I was in one of the bathroom stalls when I heard Jared talking to Paulo.

"She's a total tease. All she's let me do is squeeze her tits a few times. *Outside* her clothes."

My heart stopped. *Maybe he's talking about someone else.* But then I thought, *How would that be better?* I peered through the crack in the door. I could see their bare bums in the change area.

"Why do you keep seeing her?"

"Have you looked at her? She's hot. Besides, I love a challenge. I'll break that bitch down."

I felt sick to my stomach. I didn't know what to do. I mean, I really did not know what to do.

So I asked the only person I could think of.

"What exactly did he say?" Phoebe asked. We'd just got on the SkyTrain after kicking some mathletic butt at a school in Burnaby.

"I'd rather not repeat it," I said. "But it was really crude. And really mean."

Phoebe thought about it for a while. We were sitting next to each other, and I tried not to think about the fact that our knees were touching. "If you talk to Ashley, it could backfire," she said. "She might not believe you. She might shoot the messenger. But at the same time, you have to do *something*." She fell silent again, thinking. "My best recommendation? You should talk to *him*. Man to man."

Except I am not a man. I am a lilliputian, and he is a giant, I thought. But it was good advice, even if it was also terrifying.

We had a home game the following day. I waited for Jared outside the change room. Even though I'd barely touched my lunch, I felt like I was going to puke.

Finally he appeared, striding toward me. "Jared, could I talk to you for a second?" My voice cracked.

"Sure thing, Stewie." He pushed open the change room door.

"It's Stewart," I said. "And not in there. In private."

We walked to the far end of the corridor.

"What's up?"

I took a deep breath. *If he wanted to,* I thought, *he could squash me like a bug.*

"I overheard what you said about Ashley in the change room the other day."

"What? What'd I say?"

"That she was a tease."

He laughed. "She is."

"And that she's only let you squeeze her you-know-whats."

"Also true."

"But—that stuff is *private*. It's between you and her."

"Big deal. I just told Paulo."

"And you called her a bitch."

"Dude. I wasn't dissing your sister. It's just the way guys talk to each other."

"Not all guys. I would never talk that way about a girl I liked. Or *any* girl."

Jared smirked. "But, Stewie, you don't really count."

"Why don't I count?"

"Well, look at you. How can I even be sure you're a guy?"

"You're trying to change the subject."

"You're more like, I dunno . . . an elf. Or a gnome. Sexless. Or maybe you're one of those hermaphrodites."

I confess I had to look up that word on my computer when I got home. And I am not. A hermaphrodite, I mean.

"This isn't about me. This is about Ashley." My voice was shaking. "I just don't think you should talk about her that way."

Jared stared at me for a few moments. "I get it. You're jealous."

"Of what?"

"You have the hots for your stepsister, don't you? Gross, Stewie, that's verging on incest."

"I *do not* have the hots for Ashley!" I shouted, and a couple of kids looked in our direction. I could feel my face flush hot with anger.

Jared just laughed some more. "I bet you try to spy on her when she's in the shower—"

"*Stop it!* You're being disgusting."

"I can hardly blame you, she's gorgeous—"

"*You keep trying to change the subject!*" I yelled. "Just— quit disrespecting her like that. If not for her sake, then for mine."

He stopped laughing. "Why would I do it for your sake?"

"Because we're friends."

"Right. You and me. Friends." Jared stared at me again. His eyes looked dead.

"Jared, get into uniform now! And, Stewart, get into the bulldog suit!" Coach Stellar yelled from the other end of the hall. "Quit dawdling! Game starts in ten!"

"We'd better get a move on, Stewie," Jared said.

"Please stop calling me Stewie."

"Sure thing," he said as he headed to the change room. "Stewie."

I had to stay where I was and just breathe for a moment. I now knew, beyond a shadow of a doubt, that Jared was *not* a quality human being.

I DIDN'T TELL MY mom any of these things. And I am relieved that November is officially over for another year.

ASHLEY

WHEN LAUREN ASKED ME on Monday how Saturday night had gone, I flashed my best secretive-yet-knowing grin and told her, "Fantastic." We were hanging out on the front steps of the school, our coats pulled tight around us because it was freezing. Yoko, Amira, Lindsay, and Claudia were there, too.

"What'd you guys do?" Claudia asked, rather boldly if you ask me.

I giggled. "Oh, a little bit of this . . . a little bit of that . . ."

"C'mon, details!" Lauren begged.

"I never kiss and tell." I took out some cherry-flavored lip gloss and started applying it.

"Does he really live in a mansion?" asked Claudia. She blew a huge bubble with her wad of gum.

"Yes."

Lauren sighed. "You're such a lucky duck. I bet it was incredibly romantic."

I just smiled. But inside I felt kind of barfy.

I could never tell them the truth.

JARED HAD TEXTED ME late Saturday afternoon, two weeks after our movie date. We'd seen each other a lot since then, but always in public or around other people. This time he asked if I wanted to come over to his place. I texted back *yes*. Mom was out emceeing another fund-raiser, so I went downstairs and told Leonard my plans. He was in the living room practicing some of his fencing moves, complete with the sword-thingy.

"Will his parents be home?" he asked.

"Of course," I said, even though I had no idea.

"And your mom would be okay with this?"

"Yes."

"Where does he live?"

"Shaughnessy."

"Ooh. Fancy. How are you getting there?"

"Bus."

"I'd rather drive you."

"I'd rather bus."

"Nope. I'm driving you. Nonnegotiable."

I did *not* like him talking to me like he was my parent. But I didn't want to rock the boat, so I simply said, "Fine."

At seven o'clock, Len drove me to Shaughnessy. He was right—it is a very fancy neighborhood, very *old money,* with enormous houses. We almost got lost a couple of times 'cause the roads in Shaughnessy are twisty-turny.

When we finally found Jared's place, Leonard whistled. "Wow." It was at least three times the size of our house. There was a semicircular driveway out front and a three-car garage. It was all brick and ivy, and the yard was huge.

I was worried that Len might try to walk me to the door, so I leapt out of the car. "Thanks!"

"I'll pick you up at curfew!" he shouted out the window.

I walked up to the house. I felt really nervous all of a sudden, and my stomach started to burble in an embarrassing way. I rang the bell.

Jared answered, looking adorable in dark gray pants and a fitted black T-shirt with a thin white cardigan over top. I'd worn my favorite skirt, a short, flouncy purple number with a simple yet elegant black cotton top and tights to keep my legs warm. Jared waved at Leonard, who was still sitting in his car. Leonard waved back and drove away. "C'mon in," he said.

"Are your parents home?"

"God, no. I wouldn't have invited you over if they were."

"Why? Do I embarrass you?"

"No. *They* embarrass me. They're nothing like your folks—trust me." He grabbed my hand. "Let me give you a tour."

So he walked me through the house. There were dark hardwood floors and dark-painted walls and lots of dark furniture, which made it all, well, very dark. There was—honest to God—a billiard room. Also a library. I started giggling.

"What's so funny?"

"I keep expecting Colonel Mustard to appear, holding a bloody candlestick."

"Oh. Ha-ha," he said. Then he took me to the basement to see the indoor lap pool. Yes, that's right, an *indoor lap pool*!

We returned to the kitchen, which had gleaming countertops and fancy appliances and beautiful copper pots and pans hanging everywhere. "Your parents must love to cook."

Jared laughed. "Hardly. We have a cook who comes in twice a week and preps a bunch of meals. This stuff is all for show. My parents are all about appearances." He opened the fridge. "You want something to drink?"

"Sure."

"Beer? Wine? Rum and Coke?"

"Um. Maybe just the Coke."

"C'mon. Relax. I'm having a beer."

"Won't your parents mind?"

"They'll never know. They have an epic supply of booze."

I didn't want to seem like a prude, so I said, "How about a white wine spritzer?" because that's what Anastasia is always drinking on one of my soaps.

Jared opened a bottle of white wine that was in the fridge and poured me a very big glass, leaving hardly any room for sparkling water. He got himself a beer and said, "Let me show you around upstairs."

So I took my glass and followed him, having a few sips along the way. I felt quite sophisticated, even if I didn't love the taste.

"This is my parents' bedroom," he said, showing me the master suite. It was as big as our entire second floor. Everything was white: the duvet cover, the pillows, the carpet, and the curtains. It was the only un-dark room in the house. "And here's my room," he said when we reached the other end of the long hallway.

Jared's bedroom wasn't as big as his parents', but it was still twice the size of mine. The color scheme was lots of browns and navy blues, and his curtains and even his bedspread had little sailboats on them.

"Do you sail?"

He nodded. "We belong to the Yacht Club. Mom decorated my room in a nautical theme about five years ago. Guess I'm due for a change, huh."

"I don't know. . . . I think it's kind of cute." I couldn't help it; I was imagining a future where Jared and I would belong to the Yacht Club together. We would look so good in navy-and-white stripes and matching boat shoes!

Jared sat on the edge of his bed and patted the spot beside him. "Sit."

I smiled flirtatiously. "I'm not a dog."

He grinned. "You definitely are not. C'mon, sit beside me. Please."

So I did. We were facing two shelves full of sports trophies, all from his old school. "You must be a really good athlete."

"Yeah, we had great sports teams at St. Pat's. Borden's teams are so lame."

"Do you wish you still went there?"

"For some stuff, yeah. But the principal's a total jerk."

"What happened?" I asked, stroking his hand in a caring way. In my head I was picturing our wedding day; it would be a very expensive yet elegant affair.

"Told you already."

"You told me you dealt with someone who needed to be dealt with. But you never told me details."

He sighed and took a swig of beer. "This guy on our football team—turns out he's a homo. But he didn't tell us till the end of the season, after we'd been naked around him a million times. A lot of the guys were pissed, me included. Then I saw him looking at my junk after our final game, so I punched him. Any of the other guys would've done it, too. *He's* the one who practically committed sexual assault, and I'm the one who got kicked out. Stupid faggot."

I wasn't sure I'd heard correctly. How could such an ugly word come out of such a beautiful mouth? I thought about my dad, and I wanted to say something. But I don't know. I didn't want to get into an argument. It was just a word. As for the punch, maybe the guy had kind of deserved it. I mean, I wasn't there, right? Maybe he'd been creepy and inappropriate. So all I said was "Oh."

We were quiet for a moment. He polished off his beer, and I had another sip of my wine "So. What do you want to do?" he asked.

"We could go watch something on TV." I'd seen their enormous entertainment room in the basement. I started to get up, but he grabbed my hand and pulled me back down.

"Sure," he said. "In a while." He started stroking my arm. "You're so hot, Ashley." He leaned in and kissed me with his beautiful, soft mouth, which I liked. He's a good kisser.

Then he pushed me down on the bed and climbed on top of me.

He started pulling my shirt up. I wasn't totally against

this in theory, but I didn't like the way he was doing it. I grabbed his hand, but he kept yanking.

"C'mon, Ash, I'm dying here." I could feel what he was talking about; it was pressing into my leg.

"Jared, stop it."

I tried to move, but he pinned my arms down. When I looked at his face, it was as if he'd gone somewhere else. It was like I wasn't even there.

"Please, Jared," I said, and it came out as a whimper. "Let me up."

But he wasn't listening. He was pulling at my shirt and my skirt at the same time. "Jared, stop!"

I was starting to truly freak out when suddenly I heard "¿Qué pasa?"

I turned my head. Standing in the doorway was a short woman with long black hair. Jared rolled off me, and I jumped up from the bed. "What are you doing here?" he said.

"I live here, Mr. Man. And your mother say no company," the woman said, hands on her hips. She saw my wineglass and Jared's beer and picked them up. "I tell your parents you drink their booze." She turned her steely gaze on me. "You go now," she said. Then she turned back to Jared. "I give you five minutes, Mr. Man. I wait downstairs." She walked away.

"Who was that?" I asked.

"Consuela. Our housekeeper. God, I hate her."

I didn't hate her. In fact, right now I kind of loved her. I tucked my shirt back into my skirt. "Well, I'd better go—" I stopped midsentence. Because suddenly I saw, sitting on his desk in the corner, two figurines.

Dopey and Bunnykins.

"What are those doing there?"

Jared shrugged. "I took them as a joke. To see if he'd notice."

"Oh, he noticed. He thinks *I* took them."

"Oops." He smirked.

"It's not funny, Jared. Those were his mom's. His *dead* mom's."

"It's no big deal. I was going to put them back next time I came over."

"Why don't I save you the trouble?" I grabbed the figurines off his desk and put them into my bag. Then I hurried down the stairs. Consuela was waiting in the foyer, her arms crossed over her broad chest. She glared at both of us as she opened the door.

"I'll walk you to the bus stop," Jared started.

"No, I'm fine." To Consuela, I blurted, *"Gracias,"* the only Spanish word I know. Then I hurried out the door and bolted down the driveway.

It took me a while to find a bus stop. I didn't want to call Leonard. I didn't want to talk to anyone.

I think it was the cold that made me shake the whole way back.

Leonard was surprised to see me home so early. Stewart was, too. He had his little friend over, Alabaster or whatever his name is, and they were working on Stewart's electric bike in the basement, laughing and having a grand old nerdy time.

The family room was empty, so I slipped the figurines back onto the mantelpiece. Then I went upstairs and got into my jammies.

"Ashley?" I looked up. Leonard was standing in my doorway. "Everything okay?"

"Sure. Why wouldn't it be?"

He didn't look convinced. "Well. If you need anything, I'm downstairs." He started to close my door.

"Can you leave it open?"

"Oh. Sure thing."

A few minutes later, Shoe Horn wandered in, and for the first time ever, he leapt onto my bed. Even though he is spectacularly ugly, I was happy to see him, so happy I almost started to cry. He curled up in my lap, and I petted him and petted him and he purred and purred, and finally I did let myself cry a little bit because I wasn't one hundred percent totally absolutely positive that I wanted to be Ashley Anderson-Mitchell after all.

"WHAT HAPPENED AFTER HE toured you through the house?" Lauren kept up with the twenty questions as we headed inside.

"He lit a fire, and we sat on a bearskin rug. . . . He even poured us a bit of his parents' wine." Only the wine part was true; the rest was another scene from my favorite soap.

"And then?" Claudia asked, her mouth hanging open ever-so-slightly in a very unattractive way. I could tell she was hungry for gossip. Whatever I told her would spread like wildfire throughout the school, so I chose my words carefully.

"He has lovely soft lips."

They all squealed with delight like I knew they would.

I DIDN'T WANT TO see Jared. He'd texted me a couple of times on Sunday, but I hadn't answered.

I'd had this image of him, which he had kind-of-not-quite-totally-but-still-partly wrecked on Saturday night. I mean, I know I haven't exactly been waving the rainbow-colored flag on behalf of my dad, who I'm still mad at for totally ruining my life, but I'd never, ever want him to get called horrible names or get beat up for who he is.

And then there was the look on Jared's face when he was on top of me. Like he didn't even see me anymore.

Half of me thinks I should walk away now.

But the bigger half of me thinks maybe I'm overreacting. I mean, maybe that kid at his school really was a pervert. And as for what happened in his room, well, guys get carried away when it comes to that stuff, right? Also, I'm pretty sure he was just about to hear what I was saying to him and stop.

The thing is: he's so perfect in every other way. And usually he is very sweet to me. Maybe I can change the not-so-nice stuff over time. Men change for the better thanks to the love of a good woman all the time in the movies, so why not in real life?

I mean, we look *so good* together!! Like we could be on the cover of a magazine!! Do I really want to throw that all away over one slightly creepy night?

* * *

WE ARRIVED AT OUR lockers. Lauren saw it before I did. "Oh. My. God!" she said. Then I saw it, too: a single red rose, sticking out of the slats of my locker door.

I pulled it out. A note was wrapped around the stem. *Sorry about Saturday,* it read. *Crazy about you.*

Lauren and Claudia tried to read the note over my shoulder. I covered the *Sorry about Saturday* part with my thumb and let them read the bottom half.

"Omigod, you are sooooooo lucky!" Lauren shrieked.

And for the most part, I had to agree with her. I *am* lucky. Although during English, a thought struck me.

Is he sorry for the way he behaved? Or is he sorry that his housekeeper interrupted us?

STEWART

I HAD ALISTAIR OVER for another sleepover this weekend, and, as per usual, it was awesome. We made a lot of progress on the electric bike, and after that we played *Settlers of Catan* in my room for a good two hours. At around nine o'clock, I went down to the kitchen to get more snacks and ran into Ashley.

"You're home early," I said.

"How's that any of your business?" she snapped. Then she poured herself a glass of water and went upstairs.

If I were to create a graph representing my moods in a twelve-hour period and Ashley's moods in a twelve-hour period, with ten being "over the moon" and one being "totally depressed," it would look something like this:

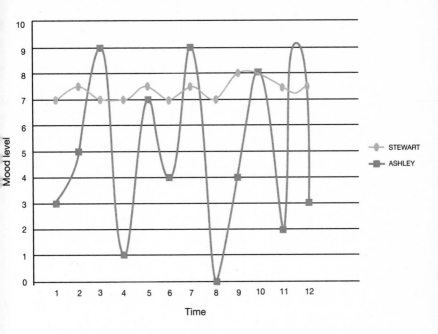

I have sometimes wondered if perhaps she has a personality disorder that needs to be treated. I even suggested this privately to my dad once, but he shook his head and said, "I'm pretty sure that's just Ashley."

ON SUNDAY, AFTER A massive blueberry-pancake breakfast courtesy of my dad (and after we had put all the plates into the dishwasher so Caroline wouldn't have a heart attack), Alistair and I went Christmas shopping. We both hate shopping, so we decided to try to buy everything we needed in one place. And because we were on tight budgets, we decided that our first stop should be the thrift store on Main Street.

We hit the mother lode. I bought:

For Caroline, her very own Royal Doulton figurine! It's a statuette of a boy fishing, and you can hardly notice that one of his hands is missing. Price: $5.

For Dad, an eye-catching navy tie with yellow and red penguins all over it. Price: $4.

For Alistair, when he wasn't looking, I found a travel chess set with all the pieces. Price: $5.

For Phoebe, I found a brooch in the glass display case by the counter. It's a unicorn! It's made of brushed metal, and it's painted purple and yellow. I am sure she will love it. Price: $8. But Phoebe is worth it.

For Ashley, I finally settled on a fluffy gray-and-white pair of cat slippers. The cat faces have whiskers and everything. Because they look brand-new, they were my most expensive purchase. Price: $10.

Total cost: $32 plus tax.

This meant I had money to spare, so I decided to call Phoebe on my cell to see if she'd like to join us for lunch. "Is it okay if Violet comes?" she asked. "I'm at her place."

"Sure. We'll pick you up."

She gave me Violet's address, and Alistair and I walked to her house, which was just a few blocks away on the other side of Main. It's much older than our modern one, and very purple. I liked it immediately because it reminded me of our place on the North Shore.

We waited in the foyer while Violet put on yet another different pair of Converse shoes. Her mom and her sister were out shopping, but she introduced us to her mom's "brand-new husband." He wore a red-and-green Christmas sweater with Santa's reindeer on the front.

"I'm Dudley. Dudley Wiener," he said, giving us both a firm handshake.

"For the record," Violet said, "none of us took his last name."

When he found out we'd been Christmas shopping, he said, "What do you call people who are afraid of Christmas?"

"I don't know," I said.

"*Claus*trophobic." Alistair and I laughed; there really is nothing like a good pun.

Violet pursed her lips. "Don't encourage him."

As we walked back over to Main Street and King Edward, I said, "Your stepdad seems nice."

Violet shrugged. "He's okay. What can I say? I am resigned to my fate. How about you? Do you like your stepmom?"

"Well, technically she's not my stepmom, because they're not married."

"But they probably will be, one day."

My heart started pounding. As naïve as it may sound, I hadn't really thought ahead to that possibility. Two things my mom could still lay claim to were (1) being Leonard Inkster's one and only wife, and (2) being Stewart Inkster's one and only mom. The second would never change, but the first one definitely could. Even though I wanted us to be a real family, I wasn't sure how I felt about wedding bells. But all I said to Violet was "Caroline's nice. She tries hard."

We arrived at Helen's Grill. I treated everyone to the all-day breakfast, which I wolfed down in spite of having eaten a stack of pancakes just a few hours earlier. Once our plates were cleared, Alistair and Violet got up to use the bathroom. Phoebe and I were left alone in the booth.

"Did you talk to Jared?" she asked.

"I tried. It didn't go very well."

"I did some research. I have a friend whose cousin goes to St. Pat's. Apparently Jared was kicked out for beating up a student because he was gay."

I felt nauseated all of a sudden. It could have been the massive wad of food in my digestive tract, but I didn't think so. "Are you sure there wasn't another reason? Like an argument they had or something?"

Phoebe shook her head. "I don't know. I don't think so. My friend says it was premeditated. Jared waited outside the school and ambushed him. The guy had to go to the hospital. He had a couple of broken ribs and a concussion."

"But you can't be positive, right? It could be a case of broken telephone."

"It could." But she sounded doubtful.

Violet and Alistair returned. I paid at the counter and we all stepped outside, putting up our hoods because it was starting to rain. "I have a French horn lesson," said Phoebe.

"And I'm meeting Jean-Paul," Violet added. "Thanks a lot for lunch." The two of them headed east.

A lot of thoughts were churning through my head as Alistair and I walked back home. But one thing had become crystal clear.

It was time to tell Ashley everything I knew.

* * *

AFTER ALISTAIR GOT PICKED up, I found Ashley lying on the couch in the family room, flipping through a fashion magazine. *To Kill a Mockingbird* was on the coffee table, untouched. "Ashley," I started, "I need to talk to you—"

Then I saw them.

Dopey and Bunnykins. Back on the mantel.

"So you *did* take them," I said.

"What are you talking about?"

"You know what I'm talking about. You stole my mom's figurines."

"Did not, nerd-face."

"Did too!"

"Did not!"

It went on like that for a while. My old Model UN Club would have been ashamed.

When I lived on the North Shore, I would sometimes babysit our neighbor's three-year-old, Amelia. She was adorable. She loved to play hide-and-seek. I would count to ten, and when I opened my eyes, she'd still be right there in front of me, but with her hands over her eyes, as if that made her invisible.

Ashley reminded me of Amelia. The evidence was right there in front of us, and she was denying it. But unlike Amelia, it wasn't remotely adorable, or cute; it was infuriating. "You are such a liar!" I shouted.

"I am not, you freakazoid! Now get lost!"

So I did. I stormed out of that room without telling her a thing.

She and Jared deserved each other.

ASHLEY

I LOVE CHRISTMAS HOLIDAYS. I mean, I really, really, *really* love Christmas holidays. It's the best time of the year. What's *not* to like? No school for two whole weeks; sleeping in; the hustle and bustle of downtown, all the beautiful lights; even the Christmas music! I could listen to "A Holly Jolly Christmas" twenty million times in a row and never get sick of it. There are also our Christmas traditions: Mom and I always spend a day shopping downtown, and we always have high tea at the Hotel Vancouver, and I let myself eat all the little sandwiches and cakes, and I don't even care if I bloat.

And I'd be totally one hundred percent lying if I didn't admit that I also love the presents! I love buying them for other people; I put *a lot* of thought into it. But mostly I love opening them! Anyone who says "It's better to give than to receive" is just trying to look good. Receiving is way more fun.

Of course, Dad's newly discovered gaiety put a damper on last Christmas. Mom insisted we invite him for dinner, and even though he gave me some amazing, spot-on gifts, I was determined not to say a word to him, so it made for a long, awkward evening.

This year, Christmas Day will be even worse. Not only will it be our first Christmas with Lenny and Squiggy, but it will also be our first Christmas with Dad *and* his boyfriend. Yes, that's right: Mom has invited Michael to come to dinner, too.

I know that on the very first Christmas a cruel king forced people like Mary and Joseph to travel a long way on a donkey just to pay taxes. And I know that there was no room at the inn, and poor Mary had to have her baby in a stable full of pigs and goats and chickens. But on the bright side, they got a famous kid out of it, right? *My* Christmas Day won't have a bright side.

Still, there's a lot of Christmas holiday that isn't Christmas Day, and when the bell rang on the last day of school, I felt pretty excited and also relieved. We'd received our report cards the week before, and I only had two As, one in home economics and one in phys ed. Every other course was a C or a D. English was marked "incomplete" because I still owed Mrs. Donnelly a new essay on *To Kill a Mockingbird.*

For the first few days of break, I mostly slept in and used

my sewing machine to update some of my clothes. It's amazing what changing a hemline or a neckline can do to recharge your wardrobe.

Mom and I had our downtown day, just the two of us. I got the most brilliant gifts for everyone: a pair of burgundy leather gloves for Mom; a basic black sweater for Leonard; a purple pocket square for my dad, which will look spectacular with not just one but two of his suits; and some silver hoop earrings for Lauren. After high tea, Mom reminded me I still had to get something for Stewart.

"Do I have to?"

"I'm not even going to dignify that with an answer."

In the end, I got him a book. It's called *How to Tell If Your Cat Is Plotting to Kill You.* I figured he'd get a kick out of it.

I also got Jared a gift, even though I wasn't totally sure where we stood. Since he'd slipped the rose into my locker, we'd hardly had any one-on-one time 'cause he'd had so many basketball tournaments and practices.

Then, on Monday—the day after Mom and I had gone shopping—the doorbell rang. I answered it in my Lululemon pants and top, straight from doing yoga with Mom.

Jared stood on the doorstep, holding a bouquet of flowers. "They're beautiful," I said, reaching for them.

"They're not for you. They're for your mom. This," he said, taking a jewelry box from behind his back, "is for you."

Mom was so impressed with the flowers that she let us go to my bedroom to do a gift exchange, as long as we kept the door open.

We perched on my bed. I gave him his gift first: a dark

gray wool scarf speckled with tiny flecks of white like snowflakes and a matching hat, from Topman. They looked fantastic on him, which I, of course, knew they would.

Next I opened the carefully wrapped jewelry box. Inside was a silver necklace with two intertwined hearts. I felt totally one hundred percent overwhelmed with emotion. "Jared, it's beautiful."

"Let me put it on for you." While I held my hair back, he did up the clasp. Then he kissed my neck. It gave me tingles all over.

I knew what this necklace meant. It meant that we were now officially exclusive. Or, as my mom would say, using one of her quaint expressions from the Olden Days: We were *going steady*.

"My folks are taking me to Whistler over Christmas. But I'll be home by New Year's Eve. . . . Can we get together then?"

"For sure."

Jared and I kissed for a long time after that, and it felt so good. Any lingering doubts I had about him disappeared. All I kept thinking was *I am in love, I am in love, I am in love.*

Oh, and also, *Our children will be so gorgeous!*

Christmas Day arrived, and I got up at seven a.m. because I can never, ever sleep in on Christmas. Stewart was already in the family room; he'd been up since six. "I spent an hour under my mom's afghan, with Schrödinger," he told me. "Just thinking about her and telling her I love her, and singing her a couple of her favorite Christmas carols."

"You're weird," I said, but not in a harsh way.

Lenny and Mom were still sleeping, so Stewart and I

checked out the presents under the trees (they had split them evenly between his ugly, fake tree with the hideous ornaments and our gorgeous Douglas fir, which smelled heavenly and was decorated in white and gold). I think Stewart enjoys Christmas as much as I do because he didn't bat an eye when I started picking up boxes with my name on them and shaking them; in fact, he sat down beside me and joined in.

Finally, at eight-fifty, we started blasting Christmas music so Mom and Len would get up. Mom made us have breakfast first. She made a delicious baked egg dish, which took *forever*. Finally, by ten-thirty, we were all in the living room in our pajamas, opening presents. Naturally, everyone loved mine.

I got a good haul, too. Leonard got me a subscription to *Vogue* magazine. I have to admit, that was pretty cool. My mom gave me some clothes, with the gift receipts enclosed in case I wanted to exchange anything (I will exchange everything). Stewart gave me a pair of cat slippers that were surprisingly cute. I'd already slipped them onto my bare feet when he said, "I bought them at the thrift store on Main Street."

I shrieked and pulled my feet out. "They're used??"

"Only gently."

"Ewwwwww!"

"Ashley, for heaven's sake. We can throw them in the washing machine if it'll make you feel better," my mom said.

Lenny got my mom a romantic getaway, just the two of them, at a fancy spa on Vancouver Island over New Year's. Mom got all misty-eyed and kissed him on the lips, right in front of us. I'm pretty sure there was even some tongue action. Stewart and I looked at each other and rolled our eyes.

"How long will you be away?" Stewart asked.

"Just two nights," Leonard said. Then he added, his gaze on Stewart, "Is it okay with you?"

"Of course it's okay with him," I said.

But Leonard just kept gazing at Stewart, waiting for his response. "It's fine," said Stewart. "But who's going to look after us?"

"We don't need anyone to look after us," I replied.

"Home alone over New Year's? I don't think so," Mom said. "I'll ask your dad to come over."

Speaking of Dad: At five p.m. on the dot, he arrived with Michael. Having Dad over on his own was less weird now; since Stewart forced that first dinner on us, we'd made it a weekly thing. Once I even let him take me downtown, but only because he promised to buy me a pair of J Brand jeans on sale.

Having his boyfriend over was a whole other matter. It's one thing to try to accept your dad's gaiety in theory; it's another thing to have to see it in action.

I will say that, much like his choices in clothing, shoes, hairstyle, and interior design, my father has impeccable taste in men. Michael is beautiful; younger than my dad but by just a few years, with flawless skin. When I answered the door, Michael was wearing a pair of navy dress pants with a pink V-neck sweater over a plain white dress shirt. For a moment I wondered if the pink was making a statement, but then I thought, *No, he just knows that color looks really good with his skin tone.* I was about to tell him that, but thought better of it. I didn't want to mislead them into thinking I was cool with this. I was determined to be a bitch all evening.

But then Michael totally ruined my plan by being awesome.

What a one hundred percent total jerk.

STEWART

SOMETIME IN THE LATE eighteen hundreds, a Russian physiologist named Ivan Pavlov figured out that if he always rang a bell before giving his dog food, the dog would start to salivate *at the sound of the bell*—it became a conditioned response.

Watching Ashley with Phil's boyfriend was kind of like witnessing a unique version of the Pavlovian response. She so wanted to hate him, but everything he said to her was like another little ring of Pavlov's bell. She couldn't help but salivate.

We were all a bit nervous having Michael over for the first time. My dad talked in a loud voice, like we were all partially deaf, which is a thing he does when he feels anxious. And I noticed Caroline giggled nervously a lot for the first hour. Even though Michael behaved like everything was hunky-dory, I am pretty sure he was more uneasy than any of us because when I shook his hand at the door, it was moist, and I had to discreetly wipe my palm on my jeans afterward.

But Michael was so easy to talk to that everyone settled into a groove after a while. The best part by far, though, was watching Ashley.

First, there were her presents: a fashion sketch pad and professional pencils from Phil, and a skirt from Michael. "It's a Desigual," Michael told her. "I got it at their flagship store in Madrid."

Ashley couldn't help herself. "I love Desigual," she blurted. Then she immediately tried to cover. "I mean—it's okay."

Caroline grinned at Michael. "You did a much better job than I did. She's exchanging all the clothes I gave her."

Later, over a delicious dinner of turkey, gravy, stuffing, mashed potatoes, carrots, and brussels sprouts, Ashley took a pass on the potatoes—and so did Michael. He caught her eye and smiled. "Low-carbing?"

"Yes!" Ashley exclaimed. "I keep trying to convince my mom to try it, even just a watered-down version, 'cause it would totally get rid of her muffin top."

"Leave my muffin top out of the conversation, thank you very much," Caroline said.

"I happen to love your mom's muffin top," said Dad.

"And I love carbs," I added.

Ashley sighed. "See what I have to live with?"

Michael smiled. "Your dad's no better. You love your

pasta, don't you, Phil?" he said, turning to Phil and giving him a kiss on the cheek.

For a fraction of a second, everything grew quiet. Phil turned beet red; Ashley stuffed a brussels sprout into her mouth. Then Caroline, sitting on the other side of Phil, gave her ex-husband a kiss on his *other* cheek. "I just wanted to say: I'm so happy to see *you* so happy."

Phil's eyes got really watery, and I wondered if he might be allergic to Schrödinger, who was lying under the table hoping for turkey scraps. He raised his glass of wine and said, "And I'm so happy to see *you* so happy." We all clinked glasses and drank.

Except for Ashley. She just stared at her plate. Michael cleared his throat and said, "Ashley, I have an upcoming event you might be interested in." She didn't look up. "Twice a year I have a private sale of top-of-the-line clothes I've bought for various films and commercials, and also things I've designed myself. We're talking stuff that some of your favorite actresses have worn. And you're so tiny . . . you'd fit into *a lot* of it."

Ashley's version of Pavlov's bell was madly ringing, I just knew it. She couldn't stop herself from salivating. I counted the seconds. *One, two—*

Bing! She looked up.

"In fact," Michael continued, looking at Phil, "maybe we could get your dad to bring you down for a sneak preview. You can set aside the stuff you want before I open it up to anyone else. I can cut you an amazing deal."

It was truly pleasurable, watching Ashley's face at that

moment. Her eyes lit up; then, realizing she looked happy, she tried to frown; then, realizing she really, really wanted this opportunity, she settled for a look that she hoped was somewhere in between, but actually made her look like she was straining to fart. "I guess that would be okay," she said.

I think it finally dawned on her that trying to hate Michael was a fool's game, so she picked up her knife and fork and finished her dinner. She ate pumpkin pie, too, even though it contains carbs.

All in all, it was a very nice Christmas. Certainly much nicer than our last two, which stank. When we were done eating, Phil brought out a bag of Christmas-themed fortune cookies that a client had given him. We took turns reading our fortunes out loud.

Ashley's said, *Ho-ho-ho! Do not fear what you do not know.* It seemed highly appropriate.

Mine said, *Merry Christmas to you! Your greatest wish will come true.* And I thought that my greatest wish already *was* coming true: we were starting to feel like a family.

It was a great Christmas holiday.

Until it wasn't.

ASHLEY

A FEW DAYS LATER, Dad took me to Michael's warehouse space, and I spent hours looking through the racks of amazing clothes. I bought bags and bags full of stuff with the Christmas money Nana had sent me, for next to nothing.

Dad and Michael helped me carry all my loot up to my room. Michael and I agreed that a few items could use some added flair. "I can lend you my BeDazzler," he said.

"I've always wanted a BeDazzler!" If I am one hundred percent totally honest, I kind of love Michael, and I hope my dad can hold on to him.

The three of us headed downstairs just as the bell rang. I answered the door.

It was Jared.

"Oh. Hi! You're home early."

"Just got in this morning. Dad got called back for some big meeting." Then he saw my dad and Michael. "Hey, Mr. Anderson." He shook hands with my dad, then looked at Michael.

I didn't know what to say. When it became clear I wasn't going to introduce them, Michael stuck out his hand. "I'm Michael."

"Jared." They shook.

"Michael's a friend of the family," I said.

Dad and Michael shared a look. And yes, I saw the disappointment. *It's complicated,* I wanted to say.

"We'll be on our way," Dad said.

I followed them to the patio doors in the kitchen, feeling a twinge of guilt. "Thanks again for bringing me to your warehouse," I said. "I really, really appreciate it."

"You're welcome," Michael replied. His tone was a bit frosty. They stepped outside and headed to the laneway house.

Jared had followed me into the kitchen. He helped himself to a banana from the bowl on the counter.

"I'm glad you're back," I said.

"Me too." He kissed me, and he smelled like banana, which wasn't entirely pleasant. "We still on for New Year's Eve?"

"For sure."

"We can't hang out at my house 'cause my parents will be there. They're having a party."

"You could come here. My mom and Leonard are going to be away."

His eyes lit up. "Really?"

I nodded. "We could invite Lauren and a couple other people over, too." I still wasn't sure I wanted to be alone with him.

"You could have a New Year's party."

I shook my head. "A few people, maybe, but that's it. My dad's going to be checking in on us, and he lives right there." I pointed at the laneway house.

Then I froze.

I could see my dad and Michael in his little living room. Michael was hugging my dad and stroking his hair.

My eyes darted to Jared. But he was turned away, throwing out his banana peel. I grabbed his arm and practically dragged him out of the room. "Let me show you all the stuff I got for Christmas."

I'm almost one hundred percent totally definitely pretty much positive he didn't see a thing.

STEWART

MY NEW YEAR'S PLANS were solid. I'd invited Alistair over for five o'clock, and we were going to have an epic Risk tournament, fueled by root beer, Twizzlers, and pretzels. Then, at around eight, Phoebe and Violet were going to come over. I told them we could just hang out and watch a movie, but instead I had a surprise: we were going to have a marathon TV-watching session of the first season of the original *Doctor Who,* which Alistair had gotten for Christmas. I couldn't wait to see Phoebe's face when I told her. I also couldn't wait to see her face when I gave her the unicorn pin.

Phil left early in the morning to go skiing in Whistler for the day with Michael, a two-hour drive north of the city. He promised to be home by eight at the latest, when most of our friends would be arriving. Dad and Caroline made us a big breakfast before they left at eleven to catch their ferry. "What's up for tonight?" Dad asked as we wolfed down scrambled eggs, sausages, and toast.

I told him my plans. Ashley said, "You can't hog the family room with your nerd-fest. I'm having a few people over, too."

"How many people?" my dad asked.

"Just three. Jared, Paulo, and Lauren." I wasn't thrilled to hear Jared's name, or Paulo's, for that matter.

"Can't you all hang out together?" asked Caroline.

"Mom, please. Reality check!"

So we agreed that Alistair and I would have our "nerd-fest," aka the *Doctor Who* marathon, in Dad and Caroline's room, since they also have a TV/DVD player, and Ashley and her friends would have dibs on the family room.

Once they were gone, I did a bit of work on my electric bike. At five, Alistair arrived, and we got the Risk game set up in the kitchen. We'd been playing for over two hours when the phone rang. It was Phil.

"Stewart, hi."

"Hey, Phil. How was skiing?"

"It was great. But the traffic's a nightmare. We're still north of Squamish. The radio's saying there's a bad accident up ahead. We're at a standstill."

"Maybe you should pull off and go to a restaurant till it clears."

"We may do that. How are things there?"

"Everything's fine," I said, just as Ashley wandered into the kitchen for a glass of water. "Your dad's stuck in traffic," I told her. "He's going to be a lot later than he thought."

She shrugged. "Okay. Say hi." Then she left the room.

"Listen, Stewart," Phil said. "I love my daughter, but she doesn't always show the best judgment. I'm counting on you to be the reasonable one until I get there."

"I will."

"Thanks. I'm really sorry about this."

"Phil, it's fine. We're just having a few people over. What can go wrong?"

Famous last words.

ASHLEY

I TEXTED JARED AFTER Dad called. *Dad stuck on Sea to Sky highway. Won't be home for hours!* A few minutes later, Lauren arrived. I took her upstairs and showed her all the stuff I'd bought at Michael's warehouse.

"Omigod, you're so lucky!" she squealed. "Who is this guy again?"

"A friend of my dad's. He's a costume designer." Then I let her pick out a couple of things to keep.

At eight, the doorbell rang. Jared stood on the doorstep with Paulo—and about five other guys. "I hope you don't mind. They're friends of mine from my old school. They had nowhere else to go."

"Jared," I started, "I can't—"

"You said in your text your dad won't be home for ages, right?"

"But he could walk in any second—"

"He won't. I listened to the radio. They're saying it's going to take hours to clear the highway. These guys will be gone before he gets back."

"Promise?"

"Promise."

What could I do? I let them in. They were carrying bottles of vodka and rum and stuff, probably stolen from their parents' liquor cabinets. "You should invite a few more of your girlfriends," Jared continued. "You know, even things out."

So I called Claudia and Lindsay, and Lauren texted Amira and Yoko. By nine p.m., there were twelve kids in our house, not including Spewart, Albacore, Feeble, and Violent, who'd taken their nerd-fest upstairs.

Jared was very sweet to me, which I really enjoyed, because everyone else could see it, too. He kept putting his arm around me and kissing my hair and making me drinks. The first one was pretty strong, but the next two went down nice and easy. I knew I should eat something, but his friends had polished off the pizzas we'd ordered before I could get my hands on a slice.

At one point, Stewart came downstairs to get more pretzels. He looked worried when he saw how many kids were there. "Where did all these people come from? We're only supposed to have eight."

I looked around. There were more kids in our house than there had been half an hour ago. I counted at least thirty. But

I was feeling great, so I just said, "It's no biggie. I just had another text from Dad. The traffic still isn't moving."

"But we gave him our word—"

"We'll just make sure they leave before he gets here. He'll never know." I lost my balance. I had to grab Stewart's shoulder. "Hey, you're getting taller." It was true; I no longer had to look down at him to meet his gaze.

"You've been drinking," he said. "I can smell it on your breath."

"So what if I have?"

"I think we should ask people to leave—"

"Stewart," I snapped. "Get lost."

He got the hint and left. Jared appeared beside me and handed me a glass. "Drink up, beautiful," he said, and I did. It was my fourth drink, or maybe it was my fifth; I don't remember.

I don't remember much of anything after that.

STEWART

BY TEN P.M., IT was impossible to watch *Doctor Who* thanks to the noise from downstairs. The music was so loud the floor was vibrating.

"Someone is messing with the bass level," I sighed. "I'd better go investigate."

"I'll come, too," Violet said, a little too quickly. She was missing her boyfriend, who'd gone to his dad's in Winnipeg for the holidays. Plus I don't think she was enjoying *Doctor Who* all that much, which was inexplicable to me, especially since the Tardis was being revealed for the first time.

"Me too," Phoebe said, and I wondered if she, too, was underwhelmed by the Doctor. I was still waiting for a private moment to present her with her unicorn, but it looked like I'd have to wait a while longer. The three of us left Alistair in Dad and Caroline's bedroom and went downstairs.

I could not believe the sight that met my eyes. There were well over a hundred kids. The front door was wide open, and people spilled out onto the lawn. A lot of them were drinking. Some were dancing. Two were fighting. One was barfing on the living room rug. The wine rack in the kitchen, which had held about six bottles, was empty.

"Holy cow, Stewart," Phoebe yelled over the music as she and Violet followed me through the rooms. "This is not good."

"No," I shouted back. "It isn't."

In the family room, a few couples were making out on the couch. Another guy was trying to pose my mom's figurines to make them look like they were having sex. "Leave those alone!" I shouted. I grabbed as many as I could and shoved them into my pockets. "They belonged to my mom," I told Phoebe. She grabbed as many as she could, too, and Violet scooped up the leftovers.

I couldn't see Ashley anywhere. "Okay, everyone," I shouted as loud as I could. "Time to go home! Party's over!"

"They can't hear you," Phoebe said. "And even if they could, I'm not sure they'd listen."

"Half these people don't even go to our school," Violet added.

The three of us headed back upstairs to regroup. Alistair was perched on Dad and Caroline's bed. "Is it bad?" he asked.

I nodded. Then, with a jolt, I remembered Schrödinger.

"I have to find my cat. The front door is wide open. I have to make sure he's okay."

I knew he was probably hiding under a bed somewhere, since that was his favorite spot when he was scared. I went into my room first. There was a couple on my bed making out. "Get lost!" the guy yelled.

"*You* get lost!" I said. "This is my room!" They didn't budge. They just stopped kissing and watched me as I looked under the bed, in the closet, in the bathroom. Schrödinger wasn't there.

Next I went into Ashley's room. I was filled with relief when I saw his green eyes glowing from under her bed. I coaxed him out and gave him a comforting hug. "There, there, who's the big, brave boy?" Then I carried him into Ashley's bathroom and closed the door. I made a little bed for him with her towel. "You'll be safe in here," I said. "I'll bring you some food and water."

Then I sat down on the toilet seat and pulled out my cell phone. I knew Ashley would kill me, but I also knew I had no choice: I had to call Phil.

It went straight to voice mail. I left a message. "Phil, call me as soon as you get this. It's urgent." I thought about calling Dad, but what could he do from Vancouver Island except worry? I wondered if I should call the police, but I was scared that the only ones who'd get in trouble would be Ashley and me, since it was our house.

As I tried to plan my next move, I heard voices on the other side of the door.

"You need to lie down." A boy's voice.

"No, I don't." A girl's voice. Clearly wasted.

"Baby, you do."

Ashley and Jared.

Then, the sound of bedsprings. Ashley: "Don't push me."

Jared: "You need to sleep this off."

Ashley: "Hmmmmhmmmm."

This was followed by a good minute of silence. "She's totally passed out," Jared said.

"You sure?" A second male voice.

"Ashley . . . hey, Ashley, you stupid slut, can you hear me?"

The other boy laughed. I was pretty sure it was Paulo.

I was completely freaking out. I had no idea what they were up to, but I knew it wasn't good. I turned out the light in the bathroom. Then, very quietly, I pushed the bathroom door open about an inch.

The only light in the room came from a bedside lamp. Ashley was sprawled on her back on the bed. Her skirt was hiked up to her thighs. Jared loomed over her. Paulo stood behind him. The door to her bedroom was closed.

Jared started to unbutton Ashley's top.

"Whatchoo doing," Ashley muttered, her eyes not even opening. She waved her arm in front of her, like she was trying to bat away a fly.

"Shhhh," Jared answered. He pulled back her shirt to show Paulo her bra. It was red. "Check it out," he said to Paulo. "It's one of those gel bras. I *knew* her boobs looked too good to be true."

Then he took out his phone. And I heard *click*. Followed by another *click*.

And it dawned on me that he'd just taken photos of my almost-sister's bra-clad you-know-whats. Meaning he was probably planning on showing these photos to others, maybe even *sending* them to others, and who knew where it would end.

A combination of Twizzlers and root beer and pretzels rose up in my throat and I had to swallow hard to force it back down.

Yet again I was faced with a dilemma for which all the Model UN role-playing in the world could not have prepared me. Yet again the dilemma revolved around Jared.

And I had no idea what to do.

Then an amazing thing happened.

Maybe it was all the sugar from the root beer and the Twizzlers, but all of a sudden I had a vivid flashback, in full-on Technicolor.

I was four. Mom had taken me to a park near our house, and I was playing with a boy who was probably seven. I guess he'd figured out that I was a bit unique, because he told me we were going to play a game that was kind of like "Pin the Tail on the Donkey," except this was called "Throw the Stones at the Retard." And he started throwing stones at me. I just covered my head and took it because I was only four and I wanted to play by the rules.

Suddenly, I heard my mom roar, "What do you think you're doing?" I dared to peek through my fingers. She was standing in front of the boy; she must have run fast because, just a moment ago, she'd been on the other side of the playground. Her hands were on her hips. The kid tried to step around her, but she just stepped with him, and this awkward dance went on for a bit. At that point, *his* mom came running and asked what was going on. "Your son was throwing stones at my son. I'd like him to apologize."

"Cedric, were you throwing stones?"

"We were just playing a game," the kid said. Then he dug his finger into his nose and pulled out a booger.

"See?" his mother said. "It was just a game."

"No. Games are fun for everyone involved. Your son was picking on someone smaller and more vulnerable than him. *He* was having fun, perhaps, but my son most definitely was not."

"Lady, get over yourself," said Cedric's mom. She took her son's hand and started to pull him away.

That's when my mom picked up a stone and threw it at Cedric. Not hard, but still; I couldn't believe my eyes. "Was that fun?" she asked. Then she threw a second stone. "How about that? We all having a good time now?"

"I'm calling the cops," said Cedric's mom.

"Be my guest!" my mom shouted. But when Cedric's mother pulled out her phone, Mom scooped me up and started running toward our car. I think she was wondering how she'd explain herself to the police. We didn't go back to that park for years. But as she ran away with me in her arms, she said, "Stewart, I may not have handled that situation as well as I could have. But I want you to remember: it is *never* okay to pick on someone who is smaller, or weaker, or more vulnerable than you. If it happens to you, or to someone else, you must always speak up."

It was time to speak up.

* * *

JARED PULLED UP ASHLEY'S Desigual skirt and took a photo of her underwear. Then he put his fingers on the elastic waistband of her underwear. I'm pretty sure he was about to yank them down—much like he'd tried to yank *my* underwear down a couple of months earlier—when I walked out of the bathroom.

"Step away from my sister," I said.

Jared looked up, startled. His phone slipped from his fingers and landed on the bed. But when he saw it was me, he smiled. "Hey, Stewie. We were just having some fun."

"You're a sick, twisted jerk if this is your idea of fun," I said. I grabbed a blanket and placed it over Ashley. Then I picked up his phone. "I'm deleting your photos."

Jared's expression darkened. "Give me my frigging phone," he said. Except he didn't say *frigging*.

"No."

"We should go," Paulo said, backing toward the door.

"Not until I get my phone." Jared took a step toward me. "Don't make me come and get it, Stewie."

"It's *Stewart*. And what are you going to do? Beat me up like you beat up that kid at your old school? Send me to the hospital?"

"That faggot got what he deserved." He took another step toward me.

"You touch me, I'll start yelling."

"You think anyone's going to hear you over all the noise?"

He had a point.

Then he lunged at me. But he misjudged the size of

206

Ashley's bed and whacked his knee on a corner. By that point, Paulo had opened the door, so I ran past both of them and into the hallway. Phoebe, Violet, and Alistair were still in Dad and Caroline's room. I shouted, "Go to Ashley's room and keep an eye on her!" Then I took the stairs two at a time. Jared was behind me, but I could dart between all the people on the stairs much easier than he could. The music was blaring and the crowds were even bigger than they had been half an hour ago. There was a hole in the foyer wall. But I couldn't deal with that right now.

I wasn't thinking; I was just moving. I ran the few blocks south to King Edward. A bus was coming. I took Jared's phone from my pocket and pushed "Emergency Call." I told the operator that a party had got out of control and we needed the police, and I gave her the address. Then I tossed Jared's phone on the road.

I heard a satisfying *crunch* as the bus rolled by.

Then I walked back to our house. Five minutes later, two cop cars pulled up.

ASHLEY

WHEN I WOKE UP the next morning, my head was pounding so badly I could barely sit up. I was in bed, wearing my clothes from the night before. A bucket sat on the floor beside me, and I cringed in horror when I saw there was barf in it. *Who put that bucket there? And whose barf was that?*

And then suddenly I knew, with one hundred percent absolute certainty, whose barf it was.

Scraps of images started to form in my head. Jared handing me drink after drink. Jared pulling up my skirt. Paulo standing behind him. The sound of a *click*. I shuddered at that memory and thought, *No, that couldn't have happened. You had a nightmare, that's all.* Then I had a flash of Stewart, shouting at Jared. . . . Then Feeble was standing over me along with Violent and Stewart's friend Albacore. After that, everything went black.

I rolled over and saw another strange sight. My dad was sleeping on my bedroom floor, a quilt pulled over him.

"Dad?" He immediately opened his eyes. "Why are you sleeping on my floor?"

"Because I was worried you might have alcohol poisoning. Because I didn't want you to choke on your own vomit and die in the middle of the night." His voice cracked, and he started to cry. "I was so worried."

"I'm really sorry, Dad."

"Stewart tried to call me, but we must have been going through a dead zone. I got here just after the police."

Police? I had no memory of that, either.

He got up and cleaned out the bucket and brought me a glass of water and some aspirin. "I'm starving," I said, remembering that I hadn't eaten any supper. I glanced at my alarm clock. It was seven-thirty.

He got me my bathrobe, and we made our way downstairs. It felt like lightning bolts were shooting through my brain with every step.

I couldn't believe the scene that met me. There were empty bottles everywhere, and broken glass. There were sticky stains on the carpet. Someone had punched a hole in the wall. A puddle of barf (not mine) was in the corner of the living room, and the smell made me almost add to it.

We walked toward the family room. I heard what sounded like crying.

It *was* crying. Stewart was on his hands and knees, looking under all the furniture. When he saw us, he said, "I can't find Schrödinger. I can't find him anywhere."

STEWART

ASHLEY AND PHIL STARTED to clean up while I searched the house for Schrödinger. I tried to tell myself he was just in a really good hiding spot, because he's a master at good hiding spots. But I couldn't find him. Later in the morning, Phoebe and Violet came over to help with the cleaning (Alistair was long gone; he'd called his mom to pick him up after the cops arrived). When I told them I couldn't find Schrödinger, the three of us took the search outside, wandering the streets and shouting his name.

As we walked, I told them that Ashley had come clean to Phil and me about the text she'd sent Jared. When we checked his Twitter and Facebook accounts we discovered that he'd tweeted and posted our address, along with the message: *New Year's Bash! BYOB!*

"I *knew* he was a creep," Phoebe said.

I didn't tell them that Ashley had taken me aside at one point and asked me exactly what had happened in her room. "Do you really want to know?"

She'd nodded, so I told her everything.

"Oh my God," she'd said. "If you hadn't taken his phone . . . I don't know what to say."

"How about *thanks*?"

Her lip had trembled. "Thank you, Stewart. I mean it. If those photos had gotten out . . ." Then she'd started to cry.

Phil had decided he had to let Dad and Caroline know what had happened, so they cut their vacation short and took a morning ferry back from the island.

Phoebe and Violet wisely left before they got home.

We still hadn't found Schrödinger.

When Dad and Caroline arrived, they walked through the house, surveying the damage. We'd cleaned up the worst of it, but the carpets would still have to be professionally cleaned. The hole in the foyer would have to be repaired and painted. At least two hundred dollars' worth of booze had been stolen. And Caroline's iPad, which she'd left in the living room, was gone.

"How could you let this happen?" she said to Phil.

"That's not fair, Caroline," he said. "I couldn't predict there'd be an accident on the highway."

She must have realized this was true, because she turned to glare at Ashley and me instead. "And you two. How could you?"

"We never meant for it to happen," said Ashley.

"You will both pay for the damage." Caroline's voice was shaking. "Every last penny."

"Now, just a second here," said my dad. "From what I understand, Stewart isn't to blame. He tried to do the right thing."

"So you're pinning all of this"—Caroline swept her hand around the room—"on Ashley?"

"Stewart didn't send out any texts. Stewart didn't get loaded. Stewart tried to get in touch with Phil, and eventually called the police. Stewart isn't the one who showed a complete lack of judgment—"

"I'm not sure it's fair to blame everything on our daughter," Phil said.

"I'm not," said my dad. "I blame you, too. You were supposed to be supervising!"

Ashley started to cry again. While the adults continued arguing, I slipped out of the room and began yet another methodical room-to-room search for Schrödinger. He was all I could think about. If he wasn't in the house, it meant he was outside. He was an indoor cat. He didn't understand what cars were; he didn't understand what coyotes were. He'd be like a Happy Meal to any wildlife.

When I still couldn't find him, I told the others I was going out to search for him again. Dad and Phil offered to come. So did Ashley. I told her I didn't want her help.

Dad, Phil, and I walked around the neighborhood, expanding my earlier search with Phoebe and Violet. We called Schrödinger's name over and over. Then we decided to search the alleys. We headed down the lane that ran behind our house, whistling and shouting. "Schrödinger! Schrödinger!"

Suddenly, Phil sucked in his breath. "Oh."

My heart leapt. "Do you see him?"

Phil didn't answer. He just stared. I followed his gaze, and a truly awful day became even worse.

A single word was spray-painted in big black letters on the side of his laneway house, for the world to see.

FAGGOT.

ASHLEY

FOR THE SECOND TIME in less than twenty-four hours, the police had to come to our house. They took photos of the graffiti, and they asked my dad a lot of questions. A bunch of our neighbors came outside to see what was going on, which I admit made me super-squirmy, because now it felt like the whole wide world knew my dad was gay. It wasn't just the graffiti; Michael showed up and held my dad in front of everyone. Most of the neighbors were really sympathetic, but the Burgesses from two houses down didn't hide their looks of disapproval, and we're pretty sure they're the ones who slipped a piece of paper under my dad's door a few days later with the word *Repent* written on it.

When the police were done questioning my dad, they talked to me and Stewart. We all sat in the dining room, including Mom, Dad, and Leonard. "We understand you had a party that got out of control last night," one of the policemen said. "Any idea who might have spray-painted your dad's house?"

I'm not proud of what I did next, okay? But in my defense, I already knew that school was going to be a total nightmare when we went back. Ratting Jared out would only make things worse.

So I shook my head. "No. I can't think of anyone."

Stewart looked at me across the table with total one hundred percent absolute disgust. Then he turned to the cops. "*I* can," he said. "I know exactly who did it. His name is Jared Mitchell." He told the cops about what Jared had done at his old school. Then he told them everything that had happened the night before. And I mean everything.

Mom started to cry when he told the police about the photos Jared had taken. "That little shit," she said, which was harsh for her because she never swears. Dad and Leonard looked shaken, too. I just sat silently, my face crimson red.

I couldn't make eye contact with my dad. I felt completely one hundred percent totally ashamed, on so many different levels. Why hadn't I stopped seeing Jared weeks ago when he'd first acted creepy? Why did I have to let Stewart be the one to say Jared's name, even though I was the one who should be standing up for my dad? I still couldn't quite believe that Jared had betrayed me in so many different and horrible ways.

The police took a lot of notes. They asked if any of the photos were in circulation, because if so, they might be able to press charges. Stewart told them about the bus. They commended him on his quick thinking, but they also said that without any evidence, there wasn't much they could do. "That was so brave of you, Stewart," my mom said, and she gave him a huge hug.

No one hugged me.

We found out later that the police did question Jared about the graffiti. I know because Jared's dad called our house the next night. Leonard spoke to him. Jared's dad shouted that there was no proof his son had done anything wrong. We could all hear him even though Leonard had the phone to his ear. Leonard very calmly told him that he should have his son assessed for behavioral issues, at which point Jared's dad hung up. The next day a letter was couriered to our front door. It was from the Mitchells' lawyer, telling us to *"cease and desist with slanderous accusations"* or they would press charges.

Leonard looked like he was going to explode. He tapped out an angry response on his laptop that included the line: *If your son comes anywhere near my stepdaughter, you will have me to contend with.*

What on earth would you do? I thought. *Put on your fencing gear, shout "en garde," and challenge him to a duel?* But it felt really good to have Leonard on my side. I didn't even mind that he'd called me his stepdaughter. I helped him Google the Mitchells' postal code; then we walked together to the mailbox with the letter. Mom tried to talk us out of it, but we mailed it anyway.

I dreaded going back to school. I tried to call Lauren to see what she'd heard, but my calls just went to her voice mail, which was weird.

I spent the last few days of the Christmas holidays holed up in my bedroom and feeling like crap. Mom and Leonard were arguing a lot about small things. A couple of months ago, this might have made me happy, but now it just made me feel worse than I already did. On the weekend I helped Dad and Michael paint over the horrible word, and I swear I could feel Michael's disappointment in me. Even though he never said it, I was sure he wondered why I hadn't done more to stand up for my dad. In fact, I was sure that all the adults in my life felt like I'd personally let them down.

Even Stewart was in a terrible mood. I felt awful that Shock Plug was missing. I'd grown to love that ugly beast. But when he wasn't out searching for him, Stewart spent all his time in his room under that stupid afghan. It wasn't healthy. When I tried to suggest he get out from under it and stop moping, he flipped out and said some very hurtful things, which I guess I deserved.

Then it was Monday, and we had to go back to school. Within the first five minutes, things went from bad to worse. 'Cause the first person I saw when I stepped through the main doors was Jared.

And he had his arm around Lauren.

STEWART

WHEN I WASN'T LOOKING for Schrödinger I spent the rest of the holidays in my room, curled up under my mom's afghan, breathing in her molecules. It felt so cozy and warm under there that I would often fall asleep and dream about her. She would come to me and hold me to her and whisper into my ear. I could never remember what she'd said, but I always woke up feeling happy—until I remembered where I was.

I think my dad was worried because he made an emergency appointment for me with Dr. Elizabeth Moscovich.

As per usual, Dr. Elizabeth Moscovich did an excellent job of helping me put my feelings into words. I told her that losing Schrödinger made me feel almost as bereft as I had when my mom died, which seemed completely cuckoo.

But Dr. Elizabeth Moscovich didn't think it was cuckoo. "You suffered a huge loss when your mom died. Schrödinger could never replace your mother, but he filled in a tiny bit of the hole that was left. Now that he's disappeared, the hole's expanded again. It reawakens the pain of losing your mother. You have every right to grieve, Stewart. You're grieving for Schrödinger, but you're also grieving for your mom."

Dr. Elizabeth Moscovich is very good at what she does.

What I didn't tell Dr. Elizabeth Moscovich is that on top of feeling depressed, I am also feeling a lot of anger. Especially toward Ashley.

Albert Einstein once said, "Two things are infinite: the universe and human stupidity, and I'm not sure about the universe." Ashley's stupidity is infinite. She came into my room on the weekend. I think she was trying to cheer me up. "If Shock Plug doesn't come back, we can go to the SPCA and get you a new cat," she said.

I wanted to throw something at her head. "His name is Schrödinger. And I don't want a new cat."

"But we could find you a really cute one this time—"

"Shut up, Ashley."

Suddenly she was tugging at my afghan. "C'mon, Stewart. Get out from under that stupid blanket. All this moping is getting you nowhere, it's a mute point—"

"*Moot* point. Not *mute* point! You call my afghan stupid? My afghan is a genius compared to you! None of this, *none of this,* would have happened if you hadn't been such a complete and utter moron!"

Her eyes filled with tears, but I didn't care. I wasn't done. "Not only are you dumb as a post, you're *mean*. You're so

219

worried about yourself and your image you don't care what happens to other people. Even your own dad!"

"That's not true," she started, but I cut her off.

"And to think I was excited to move in with you. All you do is mock me. You call me a nerd, a freakazoid, just because I don't worry constantly about what other people might think of me, just because I'm *smart*. If that's what being a nerd means, then fine. I'd rather be a nerd than a coward."

"I'm not a coward."

"You are the Webster's dictionary definition of a coward," I said. "I can't believe I ever wanted you for a sister. Now please—just leave."

She left. And I crawled back under the afghan.

ASHLEY

IF MY LIFE WAS a movie, I'd toss out all the footage from the past couple of months and do a major rewrite. Jared wouldn't even have a part. Then we'd do a reshoot, and the movie would be much more uplifting.

But my life isn't a movie. Jared was in the hallway with Lauren, and he was very real. I wanted to turn around and walk back out the front doors of the school, but I knew it would only make things worse. I couldn't avoid them, or school, forever. So I kept on going. Heads turned in my direction, and not in a good way.

Lauren looked nervous when she spotted me. But she also looked like she had won the lottery. How could I tell her that she'd actually won the booby prize?

"Hey, Ashley," Jared said as they passed by. "Great New Year's party."

"Is it true your dad's—well—*you know*?" Lauren said.

"Gay? Yes, he is." Then I screwed up my courage. "I believe the word Jared would use is *faggot*."

He laughed. "You said it, not me." Then he turned away to talk to one of his teammates.

I took the opportunity to grab Lauren's arm. "Be careful, okay? He's a real creep."

She glared at me. "You expect me to believe a word that comes out of your mouth? You've been a total bitch to me since seventh grade. I don't want anything to do with you anymore." Her words were like a slap across my face.

Jared returned and draped his arm around her shoulder. Then he looked at my chest and said, "I see you're wearing your gel bra."

I wanted to kill him. I wanted to strangle him and punch him and tear out his heart all at once.

But I didn't. I couldn't even think of a comeback. Worst of all, I felt my face go super-hot, and I knew I was twenty shades of red.

I walked away. I could hear them laughing behind me.

The same thought kept running through my head: *Stewart is right. I am a coward.*

THE DAY DIDN'T GET any better. Everyone stared at me wherever I went. Word of the party had spread, and also the news that my dad is gay. But, of course, the biggest, juiciest gossip was the fact that Jared and I were no longer an item, and that Jared and my ex–best friend were.

Every time someone whispered or giggled or stared as I walked past, I couldn't help but wonder, *Are you the one who puked in our living room? Are you the guy who punched the hole in the wall? Are you the one who stole my mom's iPad?* It wasn't a nice feeling.

Worse still, a lot of my so-called friends avoided me. Yoko, Lindsay, and Amira had clearly chosen Team Lauren and wouldn't even say hi. I had been knocked down quite a few steps on the Social Ladder. I admit: It hurt. Big-time.

The moment the bell rang at three o'clock, I headed home.

So it wasn't till later that night that I found out what Stewart had done. And that it had got him suspended.

STEWART

MY FIRST DAY BACK at school after the holidays wasn't much fun, although from what I could see, it wasn't as bad as Ashley's. Phoebe and Violet were super-kind to me and hung out with me at lunch, which I appreciated. And my fellow Mathletes made a point of being nice to me, too.

I was about to head home right after school when Mr. Stellar spotted me. "Where do you think you're going? We have a game!"

I'd completely forgotten. I dragged myself to the change room and got into the mascot costume. In the gym, I stood as far away from Jared as I could.

At halftime I started to run out onto the court when someone tripped me from behind. I went flying face-first onto the floor. Lucky for me there's a lot of padding in the head of the costume, and I wasn't hurt. Behind me, I could hear Mr. Stellar yelling at Jared, who kept saying, "But, Coach, it was an accident!"

When I had finished my routine, I ran back to the sidelines. A voice beside me said, "You owe me four hundred bucks for the phone." I had no peripheral vision, but I knew who it was.

"Screw you."

"You know," he said, lowering his voice, "I came this close to getting a nice close-up shot of your sister's—"

The buzzer went off to indicate the start of the third quarter, drowning Jared out. He trotted onto the court and started to play.

I was so angry I was seeing red.

I was so angry that all rational thoughts left my head.

I was so angry that none of my Model UN training was going to help me now.

There would be no negotiating. There would be no bargaining. There would be no compromising.

This was war.

I was working on pure fury when I ran onto the court and plowed my dog-head into Jared's stomach. I was working on pure fury when, before he had a chance to stand up straight, I ran behind him and pulled his gym shorts, along with his underwear, down to his ankles.

Even without peripheral vision, I got a good view of the look on his face, and it was priceless.

For once in his life, he looked *vulnerable*.

I know I should have been ashamed of myself, stooping to his level, but I wasn't. Kind of like when my mom had thrown stones at Cedric, I was happy to give him a small taste of his own medicine.

The crowd erupted into a mixture of gasps and laughter. I pumped my dog-fists into the air. Jared started to pull up his shorts. I knew I had mere seconds before he started to chase me.

So I ran off the court.

"You're a dead man, Stewie!" I heard.

"It's *Stewart!*" I yelled. Then I took off through the gym doors and ran all the way home.

ASHLEY

WHEN I GOT THE full story later that night, I just about fell over. I knew what Stewart had done was wrong. But I also knew he'd been defending my honor, and it made me almost proud to have him in our family.

Mom and Leonard met with the principal the next day and told her everything that had happened leading up to the gym incident. *Everything.* I spoke to her, too. She was sympathetic, and she mentioned that they knew a lot about Jared's bad behavior. She even promised that she'd personally keep an eye on him. But without any concrete proof, she couldn't do much. And she wouldn't lift Stewart's weeklong suspension. She said what he'd done was still way out of line, and she had to set an example.

If I am one hundred percent totally honest, I was almost jealous of him. I would have loved an excuse to not go to school for a week, because it was *no fun at all.*

Tuesday was even worse than Monday. Wednesday stank, too.

But then, on Thursday, a weird thing happened. For every kid who ignored me, another kid made a point of talking to me. They weren't, like, top-rung types, but I was grateful anyway.

At lunchtime on Thursday, I was sitting by myself in the cafeteria for the fourth day in a row when Claudia sat across from me. She was joined by Phoebe and Violet (ever since they helped us clean up on New Year's Day, I've decided I should call them by their real names).

"We heard about what happened to your dad's house," Phoebe said.

"We're really sorry. That's awful," Violet added.

I couldn't believe it. They were being nice to me even though I had not been very nice to them.

Then Claudia said, "I think it's so cool that your dad is gay. It's so . . . twenty-first-century. Very cutting-edge."

I smiled. I hadn't thought of it that way before.

A few more kids joined us, including some people Lauren and I had labeled as Tragics. There was Larry, who we'd nicknamed Lardy. One girl, I think her name was Melanie, told me, "I have two moms."

A boy in tenth grade, Jeff, also joined us. I recognized him from home ec; he's amazing with a sewing machine. He was joined by the kid who runs the LGBT club, Sam.

"You should come to an LGBT meeting sometime," Sam said.

"But I'm not gay. Or lesbian, or bi, or transatlantic."

Sam smirked. "I think you mean *transgender*."

Melanie piped up. "It doesn't matter. We open up meetings sometimes to kids with gay parents or siblings or friends, too, as a safe place to talk and ask questions."

"Thanks."

Then Phoebe said, "We need to talk about Stewart."

And that was when I clued in. For Phoebe and Violet, at least, it was their loyalty to Stewart that had made them come sit with me. It was kind of a punch in the gut to realize that my sort-of-stepbrother—who'd only been at Borden for a few months—had better friends than me.

"We're worried that Jared's going to try to get revenge when Stewart comes back to school," Phoebe said.

"So am I," I admitted. "It took me a long time to figure out that he is *not* a nice person."

"Yeah," said Violet. "Longer than it should have."

"He trips me in the hall all the time," said Sam.

"He shouted 'beached whale' at me on a crowded bus one day," said Larry. I shook my head in sympathy. Maybe I could find a nice way to lend him my copy of *The South Beach Diet*.

Everyone started to tell stories about how and when Jared had been a jerk to them. I even told them what he'd done to me on New Year's Eve, minus the gorier details. It felt good to be able to talk about it.

"We all know this guy's a creep. So why do we feel so

powerless when there are so many of us, and only one of him?" Phoebe asked.

"Imagine if we could have protection squads," Larry said. "Like some of the characters have on *Game of Thrones.*"

"That would be so cool," said Sam wistfully.

Then the bell rang, and we all split up for afternoon classes.

But during math and home ec, my mind wandered.

Larry had given me an idea.

STEWART

BEING HOME ALONE WAS getting tired very fast. Dad took Tuesday off to hang out with me, and also to visit the principal, but he had to go back to work on Wednesday. I knew he was worried about me. I didn't think I should tell him that I felt better than I had all year (since we were only a week into the new year, this wasn't all that hard). On the one hand, I knew I shouldn't have done what I'd done. On the other hand, I was secretly proud of myself. Who knew I could be that fierce? And I couldn't help feeling that my mom would have been secretly proud of me, too. After all, this was the woman who'd thrown rocks at a seven-year-old.

I also kept thinking, *That creep got what was coming to him.*

But I also knew that creep would try to get his revenge when I got back to school. I cannot tell a lie: That scared me, big-time.

Phoebe paid me a visit on Wednesday night. She'd brought me all my homework, which was really nice of her. We sat in the family room. She said the whole school was talking about what I'd done, and a lot of people were on my side; but she was scared for me, too.

"I'm so sorry about Schrödinger," she said.

"I still go out looking for him every day. I've called the SPCA, vets . . . nothing."

"You could still find him. How long has he been missing?"

"A week."

"Oh." We both knew: a week was a long time.

She was about to leave for her Mandarin lesson when I remembered I still hadn't given her the brooch. "Wait here." I ran upstairs and got the small gift-wrapped box.

"Merry Christmas," I said when I got back to the family room.

She looked surprised. "I didn't get anything for you."

"That's okay."

Phoebe opened the box and lifted out the unicorn pin. "It's great, Stewart. I love it."

"A beautiful brooch for a beautiful girl."

She blushed. "Smooth." Then she held out the brooch. "You can pin it on me if you want."

So I did. I was very careful to pin it well above her you-know-whats. But my fingers still touched her skin. Our faces were inches apart. Before I knew what was happening, she leaned in and gave me a quick kiss. "Thanks again."

Then she was gone. And I sat there for a long time, trying to memorize the sensation of her lips on mine.

BY THURSDAY I WAS bored, and lonely. I'd finished my electric bike, and I took it out for a test spin when there was a break in the rain. It worked like a charm. But then the rain came back with a vengeance. And I felt Schrödinger's absence in a profound way. I wanted to stay hopeful, but it was getting harder; I kept picturing him in the jaws of a coyote, or under the wheels of a car.

When I saw Phil arrive home, I dashed out the patio doors to his place, dying for some company. The awful word had been painted over in white, but we still had to buy the light brown paint that matched the rest of the house and finish the job.

"Hey, Stewart," he said when he saw me. "How are you holding up?" He knew about my suspension.

"I'm okay," I said. "How are *you* holding up?"

He sighed. "About the same. I think I'm doing better than Michael. He keeps threatening to go over to that boy's house and tear a strip off him."

"I don't think that would be a good idea."

He smiled, but he looked really tired. "You and me both. Hey, I had your posters copied." He opened his briefcase and handed me a stack of eight-by-ten papers. MISSING, they pronounced at the top. Most of the room was taken up by a color photo of Schrödinger. Our phone number appeared below. "Want to go out and plaster them all over the neighborhood?"

"Sure," I said, just as someone knocked at the door.

Ashley.

Even though she'd been really nice to me all week, I still felt a lot of residual anger toward her. I didn't make eye contact when Phil let her in. "Hi, sweetheart."

"Hi, Dad. Um. Is Michael here?"

"He's coming over later. Why?"

"I wanted to talk to him about something."

Phil looked surprised. "Oh. Well, I'm sure he'll be happy to talk to you. I can call you when he gets here."

"Okay," she said. I waited for her to leave.

"Stewart and I were just about to put up these posters," Phil said.

"Can I help?" she asked.

I really didn't want her along. But Phil said, "Sure."

So the three of us bundled up against the cold and the wet and headed out. I walked ahead, calling Schrödinger's name as we walked down streets and alleys, putting up posters. At one point, I looked back and was shocked to see Ashley grab her dad's hand. Phil looked shocked, too. But he held on tight.

We turned down another laneway, one I hadn't visited in a couple of days. It was about five blocks from our house. I called Schrödinger's name again.

Suddenly, Ashley said, "Shhh!"

We stopped.

That was when we heard it: a faint *meow,* coming from an old, run-down garage.

* * *

I RAN THROUGH THE gate and pounded on the back door of the house. A guy with a lot of tattoos answered, and at first I was a little scared, but then I saw his pretty red-headed wife in the background and she was carrying a baby, so I relaxed.

"I think my cat is stuck in your garage," I blurted. "I can hear meowing, and he's been gone a long time, a whole week—"

"Okay. It's okay," he said in a calm voice. "Let's go have a look. I just need to get the keys. Amanda, where are the keys to the garage?" he asked the redhead.

"They're in my purse." He found the keys. Then all of us, even the baby, went back to the garage. The man with the tattoos unlocked the door and lifted it.

It was dark inside. "I'm sorry, the light's busted," he said.

But in the darkness, I saw two big green eyes peering out at me. "Schrödinger!"

He was wedged between a rusty old car and a stack of lumber. He did not look happy. I ran to him and gently lifted him up. He was so thin. I held him close. Tears filled my eyes, and pretty soon I was bawling. "You're alive! Schrödinger, you're alive!"

THE MAN WITH THE TATTOOS—whose name, we discovered, was Cosmo—gave us a cardboard box so we could safely carry Schrödinger home. His wife placed an old towel in the bottom. We thanked them and said we'd see them around the neighborhood. Ashley said if they ever needed a babysitter they could call us. Then, with Schrödinger carefully placed in the box, we walked home.

Ashley was crying, too. "Scooby-Doo, we've missed you so much!" she wailed into one of the airholes I'd punched into the box.

Some things never change, I thought. But I didn't bother correcting her, because I was still crying, too.

ASHLEY

WE HAD A BIG steak dinner to celebrate Shoelace's return. Dad and Michael joined us. Dad brought his famous Caesar salad, and I ate a whole bunch of it 'cause now that Jared and I are finished, I don't have to worry about garlic breath. As part of our now-nightly ritual, we did "Truly thankful," which didn't seem as barfy as usual because I really was truly thankful that Stewart's cat was home.

After dinner, I took Michael up to my room and told him about my idea. He said he'd be more than happy to help, and he gave me a hug. "That's a bold and inspiring plan, Ashley."

Then Mom came in and I told her, too, and she actually started to cry. She put her arms around me and held me tight. "I'm so proud of you."

!!!

My heart started beating really fast, because if I am one hundred percent totally honest, people don't say stuff like that to me very often.

I stayed up super-late, drawing my ideas on the sketch pad Dad had gotten me for Christmas. At lunchtime, I found Claudia, Violet, Phoebe, Melanie, Larry, Sam, and Jeff in the cafeteria, and told them what I was thinking.

"It was Larry who gave me the idea. I started thinking, why not? Why couldn't we have protection squads?"

"Protection squads?" Claudia repeated as she blew a bubble with her gum. She sounded skeptical.

"Think about it. If we can get enough people interested, we can all do different shifts."

They looked at each other. Phoebe spoke first. "It's not a bad idea. We could take turns walking with Stewart to classes, and to his house after school."

"No reason why we should just do it for Stewart," Sam said. "We could do it for other kids, too."

"I bet I can get the Mathletes involved," Phoebe said.

"I can work on the Drama Club," Jeff added.

"Ditto the Dungeons and Dragons Club," said Larry. I didn't point out that I was pretty sure he was the sole member, since it was the thought that counted.

"Bet I can get some of the volleyball team to help out, too," said Claudia, less skeptical.

"Once I have all the names, I can draw up a schedule," said Melanie. "I'm good at scheduling."

"And of course," I said, "we have to stand out. Which is why I took the liberty of designing our outfits." I took out my sketch pad, flipped it open, and placed it on the table. They gathered around for a good look.

"Wow," said Jeff. "Your sketches are great."

I wanted to kiss him.

"I like the shirts," Violet said. "You think we could get those colors?"

"I know we can."

"What's with the funny hats?" asked Larry.

"They're called *berets*," I explained. "They're French."

"So . . . why do we have to wear French hats?" asked Sam.

"To stand out!" I replied, feeling a bit exasperated. "There's no reason why we can't protect Stewart *and* look stylish at the same time."

STEWART

LIFE HAS RETURNED TO almost normal.

The hole in the foyer has been fixed. The carpets have been professionally cleaned. Phil's house has been painted a whole new color, a very attractive royal blue. Best of all, Dad and Caroline seem back on an even keel again; I don't hear them arguing anymore about what happened on New Year's, or about dishes or socks. And Schrödinger is completely recovered; in fact, Ashley says I'd better put him on a diet because he's getting fat.

Also, we've hung Mom's painting of the bowl of fruit over the fireplace in the living room. Everyone likes it. Even Ashley. And it makes me happy that we can all see one more reminder of the amazing person my mom was.

Now I think of my new family not as a quadrangle, but as an octagon.

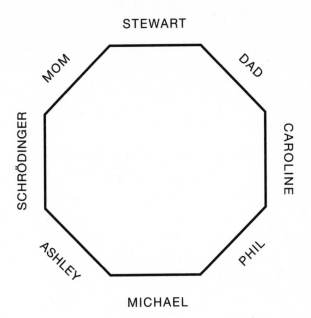

I have concluded that Mom belongs there along with everyone else, because her memory—and her molecules—live on.

I'VE BEEN BACK AT Borden for a month. Dad walked with me on my first day after the suspension ended. We went to Mr. Stellar's office and handed in my mascot outfit. Mr. Stellar told me I was the most enthusiastic mascot the team had ever had, and he was sorry to lose me. But after what had happened, he had no choice.

Then we went to the counselor's office. A lot of kids stared at me as we walked down the corridor. A surprising number of them high-fived me.

Sylvia managed to get me into a different phys ed class

for the rest of the year so I wouldn't have to face Jared in the change room. It was a start. Then Dad dropped me at my first class. "Call me anytime if you need me." He was worried. I couldn't blame him; I was worried, too.

A couple of kids in my class were wearing matching blue scoop-neck T-shirts and purple berets, but I didn't think much of it. When the bell rang, I walked into the hallway. The blue shirts followed me. A few kids in purple shirts and blue berets—including Phoebe, Violet, and Walter from Mathletes—joined them. And then, the biggest shock of all: Ashley appeared, wearing one of the blue T-shirts and a purple beret. They flanked me and walked me to my next class. "What is this?" I asked.

"Think of us as your sort-of bodyguards," said Ashley.

To say I was surprised would be an understatement.

"I hate this stupid hat," muttered Walter, and he yanked it from his head.

"I second that," said Phoebe, taking hers off, too.

"I third it!" said Violet, and she flung her beret like a Frisbee into a nearby garbage can. The others did the same.

"But it's part of the ensemble!" Ashley protested, plucking the berets out of the trash.

"Ensemble for *what*?" I asked.

She explained that the Friday before I returned to school, she, Phoebe, Violet, and some others had managed to get close to twenty kids signed up for their new "protection squad" program. It wasn't as many as they'd hoped for, but it was a start. Over the weekend, Michael helped her source the T-shirts, and they'd got them dirt cheap. Then

Ashley and Jeff went on a sewing binge all weekend in Phil's laneway house, creating the berets, which hardly anyone, it rapidly became clear, would wear.

By the end of my first week back, almost forty kids were signed up. They didn't just protect me; they escorted any student who felt uneasy about Jared, or about anyone else.

I've seen Jared dozens of times now. He doesn't seem nearly as scary, or cocky. Is this because of the protection squads? Maybe a little. He knows a lot of people—not just the squads, but the principal and the teachers, too—are keeping an eye on him. And it hasn't hurt that a tenth-grade rugby player named Darren has taken quite an interest in Ashley. He seems like a real step up from Jared: he's a genuinely nice guy who also happens to be built like a Mack truck. He was intrigued when he saw all these people walking around in purple and blue. Ashley told him what it was about, and he signed up. He also got a bunch of his teammates to sign up, so by the end of the second week, the protection squad's numbers soared to over fifty. I heard through the grapevine that Darren also took Jared aside one day and told him that if he so much as touches me or anyone else, the entire rugby team will be after him. So, while I would never say this to Ashley, Darren's threat might have had a bigger effect on Jared than a bunch of kids in purple and blue.

Still, I can't believe Ashley managed to put some of the power back into the hands of the little people. That Ashley wound up being a force for change. I told her another one of my favorite Einstein quotes: "The world is a dangerous place to live, not because of the people who are evil, but because of the people who don't do anything about it."

She just looked at me and said, "How that man went out in public with that hair is beyond me."

But she's proud of what she's done. Being Ashley, when I call the T-shirts blue and purple, she corrects me. "*Indigo* and *aubergine*."

I can tell she still misses Lauren. But I'm pretty sure that friendship is over. One day Lauren was in tears at her locker, and I saw Ashley try to talk to her, but Lauren just told her to eff off.

Except she didn't say "eff."

EVERY NOW AND THEN, Ashley and I have moments where we genuinely connect. Like recently, I helped her come up with a structure for the new essay she had to write on *To Kill a Mockingbird*. After she'd finally finished reading the book, I rented the movie for us one night. Her comment? "Gregory Peck is super-handsome!" Then she turned her gaze from the screen to me. "Hmm. Interesting," she said. "Gregory has sticky-outy ears, too. Just like you."

"So?" I asked.

"So there's hope for you yet."

And at the end of my first week back to school, she actually asked for my input on finding a good name for the squads, because she wanted to get it printed on the T-shirts.

We both agreed *Protection Squad* sounded too negative, and so was *Anti*-anything.

So I suggested a name and, miracle of miracles, Ashley liked it.

That's what's printed on all the T-shirts now.

WE ARE ALL MADE OF MOLECULES.

ACKNOWLEDGMENTS

I want to thank my early readers for taking the time to slog through previous drafts of this manuscript: Hilary McMahon, and Göran Fernlund, your thoughtful, insightful notes made this novel infinitely better. A special shout-out to Julian Miller, a member of my target audience, who gave me shockingly astute notes; he is a future top-notch editor.

To Catherine MacMillan, high school counselor extraordinaire, thanks (again) for your help. Please, please say you'll still talk to me after my son has graduated from your hallowed halls. To my friend, the amazing CBC news anchor Gloria Macarenko, thanks for answering my newsroom questions.

And my dear friends Robin Fowler and Clark and Blair Anderson: I owe you an apology. I keep stealing small fragments of your lives and sticking them in my books. In this case, I lifted your wonderful tradition of "Truly thankful."

A couple of people must be thanked twice. First, my agent, Hilary McMahon; what a lucky gal I am to be represented by the tall drink of water that is you. You are so good at what you do. Second, my husband, Göran Fernlund. You never got frustrated, even as I had to ask you to explain

Schrödinger's Cat to me for the twenty-fifth time. I still don't really understand it; I am far more Ashley than Stewart.

Almost last but definitely not least, I want to thank Tara Walker and Wendy Lamb. I'm not sure how I wound up with not one, but two of the best editors *in the world* working with me on this book. Your passion, commitment, enthusiasm, professionalism—and occasional delightful goofiness—feel like a great fit for this perennial goofball. I still pinch myself.

And to everyone at Tundra and Wendy Lamb Books who had a hand in helping this book along, I am—to lift from my friends again—"truly thankful."

ABOUT THE AUTHOR

Susin Nielsen got her start feeding cast and crew on the popular television series *Degrassi Junior High*. They hated her food, but they saw a spark in her writing. Nielsen went on to pen sixteen episodes of the hit TV show. Since then, Nielsen has written for many Canadian TV series.

Nielsen's first two young adult novels, *Word Nerd* and *Dear George Clooney: Please Marry My Mom,* won critical acclaim and multiple young readers' choice awards. *The Reluctant Journal of Henry K. Larsen* won the prestigious Governor General's Literary Award and the Canadian Library Association's Children's Book of the Year. She lives in Vancouver with her family and two extremely destructive cats.